More Praise for Communion

When writing about the modern world and our shared human condition, it is one thing to find the magic in the ordinary and the mundane; to pull, like a dentist performing an extraction, surreality out of the real. With Communion, TJ Beitelman takes an entirely different tack. His is a more nuanced more delicate style. Here he writes about our normal world normally and carefully and clearly; he forces the very plainness and starkness of his world to evoke a much more palpable sense of wonder or grief or terror in his reader. Beitelman writes in small earthquakes that, while subtle, are no less cataclysmic than their Richter-breaking brethren. He creates entire histories, relationships, townships and metropolises simply in the way a couple pumps gas, fails to tie a tie, shares a plate of sushi or reads the morning newspaper. Beitelman's great gift is in allowing his reader to experience his stories as intimately as his characters remember their own pasts: "There was a boy in second grade who lit is own right hand on fire. Sometimes in our travels I believed that this boy was me."

—B.C. Edwards, author of *The Aversive Clause*

Communion

stories

TJ Beitelman

Black
Lawrence
Press

Black
Lawrence
Press

www.blacklawrence.com

Executive Editor: Diane Goettel
Book and Cover Design: Amy Freels

Copyright © TJ Beitelman 2016
ISBN: 978-1-62557-942-3

Published 2016 by Black Lawrence Press.
Printed in the United States.

Contents

Acknowledgments

Some of these stories were first published elsewhere, often in slightly different forms.

"Arctic Circle" appeared in *Staccato*.

"Manna" appeared in *Bellevue Literary Review*.

"Resident" appeared in *Quarter After Eight*.

"Joy" appeared in *Blackbird*.

"Ruin" appeared in *Yalobusha Review*.

"Blackface" appeared in *Indiana Review*.

"Delivered" appeared as "Rooster" in *Quarterly West*.

"Yoi, Hajime" appeared in *Permafrost*.

"The Scrivener" appeared in *Bop Dead City Review*.

"Hope, Faith, and Love" appeared in THE2NDHAND.

Many thanks to the editors. The italicized material attributed to Benazir Bhutto in "Notes on an Intercessory Prayer" is taken from various video clips of actual interviews with Mrs. Bhutto that have been collected and presented in the 2010 documentary *Bhutto*. It appears here by permission of the filmmakers, Duane Baughman and Johnny O'Hara. My thanks to them, as well. And, as always, my gratitude to the fine people at Black Lawrence Press is immeasurable, in particular the eagle-eyed Gina Keicher and the inimitable Diane Goettel.

Arctic Circle

The young men and women of the high reaches of ice devised a party for themselves. In a very cold freeze, a group of ten or twelve gathered in one boy's father's barn. In amongst the smells and shuffling of the livestock, the girls dared to unwrap the bundles they'd become. As they watched them do it, the boys tried very hard to breathe, then they themselves quickly remembered to follow suit. Without those many layers, all of them were like pupae, naked in a new skin. They pretended it was summer, very far away, that one of them might, at any moment, break into a sweat. The boys fanned the girls; the girls blew cool breezes into the boys' ears. One girl, at the height of all this merriment, fumbled through her discarded parka. She found the dimpled orange globe she had buried there. When she ripped the skin, tore it off in one long, curling piece, the smell—that of a faraway, foreign summer where things are light and sweet and very warm—filled the barn. The rose-fleshed girls and the scrawny boys watched, rapt, as she took the sweet sections, one by one, into her cold mouth.

Masks

This was the game: they took turns by the black-ice creek. One boy unwrapped his carefully muffled head and turned his back to the others. He proceeded to hold his now naked head out against the blue-cold elements. His mouth curled into a long, thin grimace. The tips of his ears turned red, threatened purple. When he could stand it no longer, he brought his hands to either temple and then worked the skin inward and down. In the freezing cold, the skin had lost its elasticity. His forehead held the wrinkles. He had aged by decades. He then turned and presented this new old face to the circle of his friends, all of them presumably unblemished and still young beneath their bundles. The warm ones pointed and convulsed, delighted, and the one who'd made his face turn dead could then scramble for his coverings, blood slowly returning to warm and rejuvenate his cheeks, his ears, the very tip of his nose. Then another boy turned his back and the game started again. One boy after another. Face after face. In the relentless, impossible cold, near the very top of the world. This, a simple sacrament of defiance and resurrection.

Vows

He was a very handsome man. In this way and in others, he was a man of extremes. It was something she knew about him.

When they went to visit his mother, the old woman made them split pea soup with fatty ham hocks and she treated them like two children. There was the smell of wood smoke. Store-bought pastries for dessert. Then the long ride home along the bucolic state roads.

—*I just want to know why you said what you said.* He did not take his eyes from the road.

—*I haven't said a word for ninety minutes straight,* she said.

—*You know what I mean. What you said about the light coming in the window in the morning.*

—*My god that was Wednesday.*

—*It was Friday.*

—*Wednesday and Friday are the same thing, nearly.* She turned her head away from him and caught a whiff of her own hair: salon shampoo, traces of wood smoke. The sky was gray. The trees had leaves but not many.

—*It's a free country,* he said. *You can say what you want. But when you're with another person, in that context*—

—*Everything is pregnant with meaning.*

—*Something, yes. It's pregnant with something. I wouldn't have picked that metaphor.*

—*I think it's not a metaphor anymore. It's just a cliché.*

—*You're not going to tell me why you said it, are you?*
—*I'm almost positive I don't know.*
And that was it for a long time.

He was tired. It was almost nighttime. They found a service station at a crossroads and stopped. He rubbed his eyes and she pushed open the heavy door.

—*I have to pee*, she said.
—*You're driving the rest of the way*, he said. *I can't keep my eyes open.*
He took her silence as acceptance. Then she broke it.
—*I said what I said because I couldn't think of anything else to say.*
—*And that's what you managed?*
—*I couldn't think of anything else*, she said, and then she went to pee.
With no ceremony, he climbed out of the car to pump the gas. In the far corner of the lot, almost behind the station, three wiry young men drank beer from silver cans and leaned on a muddy pick-up with oversized tires. One of them crushed a can and tossed it into the bed. She walked in their direction, toward the women's restroom. As he pumped the gas, he noticed the dress she was wearing for the first time. This dress was wasted on a visit to his mother. A pale yellow thing, almost but not quite white. It clung close to her trim torso and then billowed into sheer whimsy around her long legs. The weather was a fraction too cold for this dress and she was not wearing her coat. She hugged herself to keep warm. Until he heard the low whistle and the accompanying muffled guffaws, he had not even seen her in this dress. The figure she cut. After she disappeared into the restroom, he found he had been holding his breath. He exhaled and returned to the duty at hand, inserting the nozzle into the tank and trying to push the moment out of his mind. A stream of pink leaked across the sky, near the horizon. The adjacent field was bare and stubbly, plucked clean of whatever it once produced. He was wide awake.

—I thought you wanted me to drive.

—I'm not tired anymore. The fresh air woke me up. I can go the rest of the way.

He twisted the gas cap until it clicked several times and took two heavy strides toward the driver's seat.

It wasn't that he heard what they said. He did not have to hear it. Young men—men of any age—achieve a tenor and a tone in the general proximity of other men. This is older than tribal. Therefore he did not need to hear the words to know in an instant that they were directed at him, as were the raucous, astringent peals of laughter that followed.

He was a man of extremes. Capable of profound silences, silences in which he disappeared completely. But a vein of intense feeling—a full volume intensity—ran through it. Or just underneath it. In circumstances such as these, he could dredge up a wholly different version of himself. He paused, stood straight, and raised both fists—middle fingers erect—in the direction of the truck. He held the gesture for several seconds, lest it be mistaken for something other than what it was.

And then he got in the car and drove away.

The last act of this particular gray sky was to break into an astonishing range of reds and yellows and oranges just along the horizon line. She found that she had—almost without meaning to—placed her slim pinkie finger on the cool, flat passenger's side window. The unselfconscious gesture of a child. Though it was, of course, impossible, she wanted to somehow touch these bright colors that had burst from nowhere and nothing.

—You'll make a smudge, he said, without looking over. Months or even weeks before, she might have teased him for being so predictable, so stuffy, and then she would have squeezed his knee or even ran her hand up his thigh, to see if she could get him to react. But now she simply allowed her finger to curl into her palm, which she dropped into her lap. With the stubby digit of his thumb, he depressed the button on the steering wheel that brought the stereo to life. Brahms. The music was too loud for her, she could not think, but he turned it up. She closed her eyes and put her head on the rest but it was too hard for even pretending to rest, and, with her eyes shut, the music became that much louder. She decided that the day had turned finally and irrevocably bad.

At first it was a persistent sense of manic, unbridled energy hulking too close behind them. He did not even bother a glance at the rearview. He kept calm. He took his foot off the accelerator, allowed the car to lose a fraction of its momentum, and then again put his thumb to work, this time setting the cruise control. They had just entered a long stretch of straight, flat road, and the enticement seemed to work. The truck accelerated, crossed the double yellow line, and growled up to pass them. He tapped the brake to disengage the cruise and the car faded back. A signal of deference. But instead of passing, the truck edged ahead just enough so that the bed was in line with his window. He tried to fight the urge to look over, but he looked. Three young men crouched there. All three of them wore broad grins on their faces. His gesture at the filling station was an invitation they accepted with what could only be described as profound joy. He turned away from them and kept his eyes forward. *They will throw something at the car*, he thought. He resigned himself to it. *Beer cans, probably.* He hoped the cans would be empty. The dents and dings would require a week or more in the body shop. This could no longer be helped. He began to construct a feasible reaction for her sake, something that conveyed surprise and indignation. In his periphery, he felt her lean forward and look past him to see what was happening.

She made a noise—a small, startled noise—and she trailed off.

Despite himself, he looked again. One of the young men had raised up, almost to his full height, as the other two helped anchor him. His black hair whipped and he squinted from the force of the wind. He had loosened his fly, and reached into his pants. What he pulled out was ropy and thick. Impossibly long. Equine.

—Jesus, he said. He pressed the accelerator and pulled forward but the truck soon matched the smooth, quiet precision of the car's German engine with its own loud American thrust.

—Slow down, she said. Let them pass.

—They're not trying to pass. It's a prank.

—No, she said, there's another car.

The sun had set and there was now just the blue pall before the full-fledged night. She was right. In the distance, a set of headlights advanced toward them. He eased his foot further into the accelerator but the pick-up surged forward with him.

—Slow down, she said.

He knew nothing good could come of this, that there was no graceful extrication. He knew that he must slow down and that, in the end, he would. Still, he allowed himself a few more seconds of rash, reckless, and unrelenting speed. She put her hand to the dash, closed her eyes. A deep thud sounded from the rear flank of the car and she let out a loud gasp. Two more deep thuds. They were throwing full beer cans. He let himself believe they were now perhaps, in fact, afraid and—he could not help it—he felt himself grinning.

—Stop it, she shouted. Stop.

The oncoming headlights were close enough now to see that they were attached to something larger than just a car or even a pick-up truck. Something big, industrial. He brought the car into a pronounced deceleration. Her seatbelt caught her slight lunge forward and pressed her back into her seat. The pick-up zoomed ahead in that instant and made an S-shaped swerve into the proper lane.

He braced for one last salvo, lobbed directly into the windshield, but it never came. Instead the pick-up motored on. Moments later, the oncoming vehicle—a passel of logs stacked high in its long bed— rumbled past. The car was now nearly stopped on the empty road. It gave a small shudder in the wake of the passing logs. A moment later, in the irrevocable stillness, it moved forward into what had become a vast but simple darkness.

Manna

The boil of his brain and an afternoon constitutional, up the long hill. His heart a flibberty-gibbet in his chest. A flapping bird. The ocular symptoms: a flutter in the middle of his visual field. Most days it is all he can do to trudge down the hill and back up again to his small house, the house he shares with Millie, who is addled, who can sometimes be mean (through, it must be said, no fault of her own: neural plaques), who he is (*after all these years*) still married to. But today. In his periphery. The bright, wet periphery following a sunshower. The black street still slick. Someone—a teenager, most likely, jettisoning contraband in a moment of: pique, panic, prescience—tossed a bag full of problems into the thick, wet grass near the bottom of the hill at the entrance to the shabby subdivision. He is old enough, near enough to his final dispensation on this earth, to believe in fate. He was meant to find it.

It is a plastic baggie full of: Swisher Sweets, matches, loose hashish, and one full hand-rolled illicit cigarette. A plastic lighter. He is not too old to know what it all means. The children today are the source of such glorious trouble, such things that he could not have imagined when he was just a boy their age, dreaming what it might be like to kiss Josephine Maldonado on the neck. What that might taste like. The feeling it might make all the way to the tips of his fingers. God bless them, these children. God bless them. He collects it. In the four seconds it takes him to stoop and grab it (the sore spot

he ignores in the small of his back; the audible pop in his left knee)
he is again fourteen years old.

Millie is a mere lump in the bed, shrouded by thin blankets, sheets
he rotates—with precision; the ritual in it—every other day. He pulls
the old chair next to the bed. There is not much light in the room.
The blinds are three-quarters drawn.

—Juice, she says. This is what she says when she means she wants
water.

He reaches for the water on the bedside table, taps her cracked
bottom lip with the straw.

—You need some lip stuff, don't you, darlin?

She sucks the water down, spits the straw when she's done. When
he applies the balm, her face squeezes. A dreadful mask. Much more
than a simple frown. She hates for him to touch her face. Not least
her mouth.

—I know, he says. Life is a hard business.

A quick pass of the tube over his own lips and then he slips it back
into his pocket. Millie's face softens again. She is awake, what passes
for alert. He would read to her now or pretend to reminisce. If it was
any other day. This day has proved itself to be unusual. He takes the
plastic bag from his pocket—not the pocket where he keeps the lip
balm, the other pocket, the pocket that is almost always empty—and
puts it on the bed. Millie is or is not aware of it. Not *what* it is, but
that it is there at all. He scoots the chair back a little, rises to crack
the window, then returns to the chair and the bag.

When he was a boy, he had a friend—a Chinese boy whose parents never spoke—with whom he would traipse into the woods,
down to the tracks. This was what they called treasure hunting.
They found railroad spikes. Once a dead raccoon, bloated and stiff.
Another time a penny on the rail, flattened into a paper-thin copper

sheet. They always found something. It was only a question of what they would find. Later he came to believe that the rest of life is not so much about what you find but what you lose instead. (What was the Chinese boy's name? That's lost now too.)

The sound of the bag is a happy, yielding sound. He pulls out the cigars and the cigarette and the lighter, careful not to let any of the loose hashish spill onto the sheet. The cigarette is stiff and light in his fingers. It is only a matter of lighting it, which he does, but only after replacing the cigars and fastening the bag again. He takes one drag and then another and then he leans into her and holds out the lit cigarette for her to see.

—Like at the dances, he says. When I'd start one for you. Like a gentleman.

Millie scowls. She rubs her balmed lips together then parts them and he brings it to her lips. She has not smoked in thirty-five years but she pulls it deep into her lungs and holds it there. The ease of it startles him. That she does not cough. That the rush of the exhaled smoke is pure and strong and alive. He is dizzy already but he takes two more quick drags and lets Millie have another turn. They trade back and forth this way for half the cigarette, ashing into her water cup for lack of a better place. The little island of gray soot floating intact for a few seconds and then spreading out and darkening over the surface.

—I say, he says, we save the rest for later.

—I'm hungry, she says. Her face is soft, as soft as it has been in years. As soft as it has ever been. No: softer. Her eyes open and aware, almost shining. I could eat, she says.

—He rises from the chair, collects the cup of water and ashes, and he kisses her on the forehead. When he leans down he braces himself on the bed to keep his balance. She smells like something more than smoke. Incense.

—I'll see what I can do about that, he says, and he makes his way through the half-dark and down the stairs.

A pat of butter, thicker than he might ordinarily use. A quarter of a yellow onion, chopped. This he stirs in the skillet with a wooden spoon. Then a large egg on top of that and more stirring. Two white slices of bread into the ancient toaster oven. Then one square slice of American cheese into the skillet mixture. More stirring to melt the cheese. He takes the skillet off the heat, pulls out the toasted bread, and puts it on a small plate. A thin, careful layer of mayonnaise on one piece of toast. He spoons on the egg, all of it, and salts it. Still it wants something. He fishes out the ketchup, taps the side of the bottle until it yields a sweet, red dollop.

It is the kind of feat—the methodical construction of something ordinary but also nearly perfect—that he might not have noticed on any other day. On this day, in this state, he feels the achievement, he wants to mark it. The kitchen faces west. Outside the sun is going down. There is something peculiar about the way the sun sets against the back of the house: just before it falls behind the horizon, it seems to brighten. For three minutes, maybe five, the backyard glows orange and red. In that short burst, there is no doubt that the sun is first and foremost a very near star, that the earth is a rock it warms.

He walks out into it. He finds that he has carried the plate with him. Her perfect egg sandwich. The warm, orange, dying sunlight. He sits on the porch step and takes the sandwich in his hands. The way to mark this is to take it in, though it wasn't meant for him. To take it in, one slow bite at a time.

Once, on the island of Guam, when he was in the navy, he went with his drunken buddies to a fortuneteller woman. She lived in something like a trailer. A small television blared in the front room.

—You will live until you are 84, she told him. You will find love. It will take time. There will be sadness. Life will be better for you after you turn 40.

Fortunetelling seemed then and forevermore like no special trick. What is to come is easy enough to see in broad strokes. Even in an empty backyard that has finally yielded to the dark:

He will rise with an empty plate and return to the kitchen, this time bathed in its fluorescent light.

He will do what he did again: butter, onion, egg, cheese, stirring. Toast.

Condiments.

He will put it on a plate. This near-perfect thing he has made. This near perfect thing he has made again. Then, again, up the stairs. The plate in one hand. In the other a fresh glass of cold water that she will call juice. Step by step. The climb he knows so well. The climb he does not, will not, even today, take to be his own ascension.

Antony and Cleopatra

Antony is the druggist. He believes this is a particularly difficult life. Cleopatra works at the fast food restaurant and studies belatedly at the community college. Hers is still, somehow, a starry life.

†

He arrives home. It is a simple place, modestly lit. There is wood paneling and a safe, musty smell. He pours a juice glass half-full with spirits and sits and stares at it in the half-light.

Antony smuggles pills home because he can. He is indiscriminate about it. He does it to pass the time. A handful of Quinidex, Propalanol. Medicines for old people. He is not, for now, interested in what they can do to him. He pulls out a pill—a powdery yellow one—and finds the potted plant on the windowsill above the kitchen sink. As if it were a golden seed, the germ of a new life, he plants the pill in a deep hole he's burrowed in the soil with his plump pinkie.

†

He has taken to driving aimlessly. He listens to AM radio, its buzzing and pops, its self-assured men talking about hellfire and quarterbacks. He turns the car when he feels moved to turn. The rest of the time he simply stays in his lane looking straight ahead, as if he belongs, as if he is going somewhere in particular. Antony drives through neighborhoods, entire communities he never would have sought out on his own. He entertains the idea that they did not exist before he drove through them. Sometimes he stops, just to be stopped in one of these new places. One time in particular, he stops at a restaurant and eats greasy fast food. He is not particularly hungry.

It is, to be precise, a fried chicken restaurant. Two workers prepare for the lunch rush.

"Cleo?"

The assistant manager—a large black man named LeRoy—carries a paper sack filled with frozen French fries on his shoulder. He calls for her again. When she doesn't answer, he puts the sack on the slippery floor and goes to the front of the store to look for her. He finds her at the register, sitting on the counter. She runs her fingers lightly over the touch-key pad.

"Get off there," says LeRoy. "We're gonna have a room full of people in here before long. Do your shift preps."

LeRoy goes back to his French fries. Her heart is not in it. Cleo looks toward the doors and hops back on the stainless steel counter. She goes to pondering the buttons with her long, caramel-colored fingers. She is lost in the keypad when Antony shuffles in, stuffed into his fleece-lined jacket.

"You don't look open," he says. "The sign says you're open."

Cleo jumps back and almost falls off the counter. Then she laughs for no reason. An infectious thing, her laugh. Loud, with plenty of teeth and even, sometimes, tears. She is trying to say "I almost busted my ass," but she can't breathe to say it. Antony is confused and blank before her, this explosion of spirit.

"I didn't say anything funny," he says. "There's nobody in here. You look closed."

Which only makes her laugh even more. LeRoy comes out to investigate, sees Cleo rolling on the counter, and goes back to the fryer, shaking his head. Cleo gathers herself, though she is still glowing from her outburst. She hops down behind the counter to take Antony's order.

"French fries, please. And an orange soda."

"Fries and orange drink for the funny man."

He pulls exact change from his pants pocket and puts it on the counter. It is the hand, its slenderness, its particular shade of brown, that catches his attention.

"Are you an octoroon?" he says.

She looks up from the keypad, just for a second. She looks younger than she really is. She almost smiles.

"I hope so," she says. "It sounds like someplace far off in the world."

Antony looks at her face, her hair, the slight smattering of freckles on her nose.

"You are. I'm sure of it."

Antony buys a *USA Today* from the machine outside and eats and drinks slowly. The words on the page slip past him as he watches the young girl behind the counter. *She is Light*, he thinks. *She is all Light.* At first, he does not know what to do with this revelation. He simply watches her take orders and smile. When he finally leaves—many minutes after he has finished his paltry lunch—she waves at him and smiles again and he resolves to come back for lunch, to keep coming back as long as she keeps smiling.

†

Antony is full but not fat, thinning but not bald. He has just the faintest strands of auburn hair on his stomach and chest and arms and fingers and toes. Cleo traces her fingers along his front because she believes this is what lovers do. He is quiet, staring straight up at the ceiling in her childish room, not quite amazed that he has, in short order, been able to get to her bed.

"How did you find me?" she says.

It is a long time until he answers—so long that she almost cannot remember her own question.

"It was an accident, I think."

Cleo's room is pink. It is the room of her youth; she left and now she has, by some unstated necessity, returned to it. There are frills, lacy things. Posters on the wall—pop bands, men with teased hair and impeccably applied make-up. The shades of her brown change and meander over her body. Almost creamy on her stomach and under her arms; coffee-and-milk on her shoulders. Her thighs are thick. Her too-small t-shirt covers her small breasts; a pair of purple panties does not fully contain her backside. Her long brown curls are tucked behind her ears. She is enough to make Antony shudder.

She pulls on a pair of sweat pants and goes to the dresser. She bends over, exposing the small of her back, its wispy hairs, imperceptible at a distance, but he knows they are there from the memory in his fingers. She writes something on a piece of paper. She takes it to Antony, who is still undressed on her bed.

"Go," she says, and hands him the paper. "Go before my dad gets home."

Antony spends the remainder of that afternoon folding and unfolding the paper, reading and re-reading the note:

Good-times Cleo—937-4150

†

LeRoy, as always, pours French fries into their baskets and racks them in preparation for the lunch rush. He makes sure, everyday, that there is never a shortage of fry baskets during lunch. He prides himself on it. Never a want for fresh, hot French fries. Cleo sweeps the floor.

"How come you always smilin'?" He doesn't turn away from pouring the potatoes, like white fingers, into the baskets.

"I don't know," says smiling Cleo.

"You smile like you into mischief," says LeRoy. He still doesn't turn from racking baskets. Cleo stares at the very dark skin of his neck. "You ain't doin' nothing you ain't suppose to be doin'?"

"Who's to say what I'm supposed to be doing?"

He turns hugging the cold bag. "That's hard talk when you know your Pops ain't likely to take a shine on you just smilin' and carryin' on 'cuz you got you some little boyfriend."

"What makes you think it's a boy?"

"I know that look. I ain't all that far from twenty-something. And I know what it looks like when somebody's up to no good. Twenty-something no-good is all smiles."

She turns away and tries not to smile but she can't help it. "Well, I'm twenty-four. Not twenty-something. And it ain't a boy."

†

"Ant?"

This is a name only she calls him. They are sitting on a bench in a park on a ridge. They stare down at the small city below them. He has left from work early, she is off for the day. Above them towers a statue of the Roman god of iron works, who lords over the city's dead steel industry.

"You know," she says, "I've lived here my whole life and I've never been up there. Isn't that weird?"

"You're young."

"You ever been up there?"

"Once, I think."

She leans into him and puts her hand through the crook in his arm. "Tell me." She is wearing a hat, the kind of hat old men wear when they are fishing. He is just beginning to take for granted this kind of silly beauty in her.

"I don't know. It's really..." he pauses, looks it up and down in the distance. "It's real high."

"Take me up there."

"I think it costs money. You can imagine it better than it is in real life. Especially you. Trust me, you aren't missing anything."

"I want to go up."

Antony stares down at the city, his usual pout planted firmly on his face. He stands and takes her hand in his.

"I'm just saying," he says, "when you get up there, I don't want to hear anything about how boring it is. How it isn't any different than you always thought."

†

The security guard who tells them the elevator is broken has the red nose and yellow eyes of a drunk. He tells them they are welcome to use the stairs but that maybe, after all, it's not worth it. It's a long way up and it looks like it might rain. They can, he says, always try back tomorrow. Antony thanks him and turns to walk away. Cleo heads for the stairs and is climbing before he can ask her to stop.

†

"We're as high as an airplane up here."

They are out on the metal walkway, out in the elements. There are one or two drops of rain and the wind is insistent. Antony is bent over with his hands on his knees and he is just now catching his breath. He tries not to look down through the metal grating and to the sidewalk far below. One small corner of the sky has turned a spectacular, gaudy pink in the considerable time it has taken them to climb the stairs. The light spills onto Cleo's face.

"I'm trying not to think about it," he says, finally lifting his head. "You do know we're going to have to walk down from here?"

"No we don't. We'll fly." She smiles her smile and spreads her arms.

"Maybe twenty-four-year-old octoroons fly. Fat, thirty-eight-year-old pharmacists don't fly."

He leans up against the stone wall and slides down it until he is sitting in a heap. She leans against the railing, arms spread, dipping this way and that, as if navigating through the air. Finally, she begins to dance around the walkway, arms wide, until she comes to Antony and hovers over him.

"You're such a cute man," she says. "I hope you're always this cute." She bends over and kisses him on the top of the head. Then she goes back to the railing and stares out until the small patch of pink fades from the sky.

"How did I find you?" he asks.

"Accident," she says.

†

This is an improbable love arrangement and he knows it. He cannot remember how it started, and now it has started and he cannot stop it. There are those it must be kept from: Cleo's father, Antony's wife. Antony's wife. He has not yet mentioned her to Cleo. He has not felt the need. But he might be falling in love with the girl and they are stealing moments of every day to be together. He is staring at the television, thinking of Cleo—the small of her back, in fact—when his wife breaks this reverie.

"Sometimes, Tony...are you listening to me? Tony—listen to me: sometimes I don't even know if you're capable of participating in the world. You're not even here among the living."

Antony gets up from his chair and goes into the kitchen as she speaks. She doesn't stop talking, nor does she look up from the TV. Hers is a well-rehearsed monologue on Antony's interpersonal skills, on his withdrawal from all forms of contact. She speaks clinically, professionally, as if these things are not, by association, happening to her.

"I guess it happens to men your age. Mother says Daddy turned into a stone after ten years. Like an alarm clock went off or something. August 4, 1962, she used to say. Of course, I'm pretty sure he was sleeping around by then, but I never would have said that to Mama."

Antony does not clear his throat, he does not choke on the milk he has poured himself. He downs it in four and a half gulps, puts the glass on the counter, and walks out of the house without a word.

†

"You're full of surprises," she says.

In the dark—the only light coming from a soft yellow street lamp across the street—Cleo's room takes on the properties of a cloud floating through the night sky. Antony feels as if he is drifting away from everything in the world. The rich, sweet smells of this young woman paralyze him. He almost loses himself in her touches— almost, except for the inescapable thought of counting pills, slowly, two and three at a time. It is the one image from his earthbound life that invariably sneaks into his time with Cleo. The boredom of it. Its all-powerful and incessant tedium.

"I really have to go. We're playing it so close."

She does not open her eyes and leans into him to kiss his arm.

"I think you should spend the night."

"You're crazy. And sweet. You know I can't."

She lies back on her pillow, eyes closed, smiling. "What makes you think they don't already know?"

His brow bends in a question.

"Everybody—my dad, LeRoy," she says. Then, as he pulls on a sock, "Your wife." At first he doesn't turn around. At first, his heart is in his throat. He looks behind him and she peeks at him, her left eye half-open. Then she laughs and laughs until he pulls her night-shirt up from her stomach and tickles her sweetly, as if she really is only a child.

†

In the morning, he wears a blue frock and counts pills until they count themselves. He is engulfed in pills and fluorescence from above. There are the fat coated orange ones, which make a sound like teeth when they drop into the plastic vials. There are yellow and blue and red ones. All shapes, several textures.

When a man asks for "prophylactics," Tony looks at him, straight in his fat-nosed face, for a full ten seconds until the man looks afraid and walks away without an answer. That man, Tony thinks to himself, is a liar. That man can't call a thing by its real name. He grabs his coat and tells the store manager that his wife is sick, a problem with her pancreas, that he will call later—perhaps tomorrow—when he knows more. He has to leave. He has to leave right now.

†

Cleo is not home. He chins himself up to her window ledge, peers into her room, which is swallowed in afternoon shadows. His muscles are not muscles. They ache and give in quickly. As he sinks back to the ground—a pathetic drop of six inches—he struggles to remember what she looks like. If she even exists at all.

It is broad daylight and he is still conscious enough to know he is being reckless. He slumps into his car, leaves the door open for a moment, his leg dangling out. Finally he pulls himself entirely in, turns the ignition and decides to get drunk and drive until the car runs out of gas. And this is exactly what he does.

†

The smoky halls of the common room in the Student Union building. Room C-130. Cleo sits at a circular table drinking an Orange Crush and eating peanut M&Ms. Her biology text sits open but she is not reading it. Instead she twirls the yellow candy package in her long fingers, leaves the M&Ms in her mouth until the coating is smooth and tasteless, until it cracks with just a hint of pressure from her tongue.

Behind her the TV is on but the sound is down. A pimply boy sits on the faux-leather couch, his hands clasped behind his neck. He watches the soundless images and he doesn't move and Cleo doesn't read, though perhaps they both should be moving or reading. Something. In four minutes, a bell will ring, announcing a new class period. Still, neither of the two will move into the late, gray afternoon. Both will sit for an indeterminate amount of time, neither one acknowledging the other, with blank eyes and half-opened mouths. Not quite bored, not quite alive, and neither will know how thankful they are for this place that requires nothing of them.

At 5:03 p.m., Cleo will rise from her table, glance at her book—a drawing of a splayed vulva—and she will close it, suddenly aware of a faint headache.

"Can you watch my stuff?" she will ask the pimply boy. He will unclasp his hands and, without looking up or speaking, he will wave in the affirmative.

But Cleo will not have seen it. She must make a single-minded run down the hall to the bathroom. There she will vomit a pile of ignominious orange foam into the sink. Later, she will remember this very gray afternoon, her headache, and then the orange, which will seem to her a very bright, almost sparkling entrance into a new kind of life. All of that and a bell, ringing.

†

"I guess I'm out on 280 somewhere. Sylacauga. I don't know. Just come."

"Tony this is insane. What happened to you? Work says don't bother coming in anymore. And who's having pancreas trouble? Because it certainly isn't me. My pancreas is fine. You should know that."

"I just need you to pick me up."

"I'm not moving until I know what the hell is going on."

"Get in the fucking car and pick me up. Jesus. Why is it so hard?"

Just after *Jesus* his wife hangs up. There is a chance he will never speak to her again. Antony goes to his car and sits in it. There is a pill in a crevice of the seat next to him. A very small, octagonal pill.

The night is cold and his car is dead on Route 280, past Sylacauga, and he is at the end of the earth. The pill flecks in his hand as he fingers it. He brings it up to his eye and then puts it on his tongue. It stings as it melts.

Later, he snaps to; he has been dozing. Fifteen minutes? Hours? He wonders if the pill will bring bright lights or visions, but it doesn't. Instead he feels nothing. An especially intense brand of nothing. "A nothing pill," he says out loud to no one. "It must have been a nothing pill." He can see his breath. Like a talisman or a sign from on high, the torn scrap of paper finds his hand in his coat pocket. 937-4150. For a good time.

†

Voices outside the car:

"Ant? Good gracious."

"I told you not to be getting into no mischief. You're lucky your daddy was still at the lanes. He'd tar you up, to get that kind of call. From this kind of man."

She opens the door without responding, puts her warm hands on Tony's face. He finally knows who it is, that it is her.

"Ant, come on. We gotta go."

"I had a dream," he says. "You were in it. You were some kind of fish."

"I bet I was a real pretty fish." She puts Tony's arm around her shoulder and motions for LeRoy to come help her.

"You brought the fry man."

"This is LeRoy, baby. He's going to help us."

"LeRoy wasn't in my dream."

"I know. Only me. Only me as a fish."

"The shiniest, prettiest, fastest fish in the ocean."

LeRoy, though he is annoyed and tired and cold, cannot help but chuckle softly at that.

†

LeRoy places his keys on the dresser in his bedroom. A drunken man lies, face down, at the threshold of his kitchen. Antony rolls over on his back and stares straight up at the low ceiling. He thinks he is in a holding cell. Antony hears LeRoy's thudding steps. LeRoy doesn't seem rushed. He moves from room to room as if it is a normal Wednesday night, as if he doesn't have a stranger in his apartment. Finally, he comes to stand over Antony, drops a sheet over him, and flicks off the light.

In the darkness, Antony doesn't move. He hears the large man sleep, smells him in the floorboards—the way he cooks, the cleaning products he uses irregularly. It is the one moment in his life that he is untethered, without any notion of where he is or why he is there. He spends the rest of the night in the warm haze of dissipating drunkenness, feeling unattached to his body. Therefore he does not dream, not of fish or stars or new lives. Through the rest of the night, he is nothing, awash in it, and he lets himself feel a strange sort of glory.

The morning is something else. The large black man steps over Antony and, though he has not been sleeping, he does not move. The refrigerator opens. The draft tickles Antony's neck. There is some manner of frying—perhaps eggs and meat. In the middle of it, Antony speaks:

"She called you LeRoy."

Nothing.

"I'd like to call you Fry Man." Antony says. He says it toward the ceiling.

"Doesn't matter what you call me." LeRoy, dressed in his uniform, ready to manage a fast-food kitchen, is in business mode tending to his eggs. "Don't matter at all." He pulls the pan off the stove and slides what's in it onto a plate. He takes the food out of the kitchen, traverses Antony, and sits in front of the television.

Antony tries again. "I'd like to call you Fry Man."

For a while, LeRoy eats his eggs and watches the early news with the sound low. He pretends, for the moment, that he will not finish his breakfast, take the plate into the sink, rouse the man from his floor, and take him to whatever future he has with the girl. He pretends he is not involved. Then, when he is done pretending, done with his eggs, he says, "Let's go."

†

Cleo, the very beginnings of a daughter inside her, sorts quickly through her things. Her father is asleep, the last essences of bowling-night beer and a nightcap Courvoisier seeping onto his pillowcase. He will be up soon in any event, because he is a man of routine and a certain kind of great strength. This is what allows her to go. She knows he will comfort himself in familiar ways: his hard work with tools, the regularity of his life's sounds and places.

She grabs a large cloth bag, stuffs clothes into it indiscriminately. It is one of the few times that she is unaware of the young men staring back at her from the posters on her walls. Their fleeting fame. The softness and smoothness of their photographed skin. They had been the evidence she needed, that there was something perfect in this world. Something to aspire to. There is no time for them now.

"Dammit, LeRoy," she says, looking out her window. "You better get your ass here."

†

LeRoy expects Antony to slump in the seat next to him, maybe rest his head on the dash. Instead, the man sits completely erect with a look of contentment on his face. Gray light slowly comes over the sky. Antony's chin is strengthened by a few days growth of beard and his impeccable posture. A date hovers in his mind: August 4, 1962. The day his father-in-law turned to stone. Maybe this is a day like that. Maybe that day has already come. He looks outside at the sidewalks, the buildings and knows that he will never leave anything in his current life. Revealing nothing, saying nothing, he will explain himself back into it.

"Let me out here."

LeRoy looks at him, and looks again. Antony has not taken his eyes off the road.

"Tell her I'm sorry. Let me out of here."

†

She meets him at the door before he has to knock. When she asks, he lies at first. He says the man went home to get some things, perhaps to leave a note.

"He said he'll meet you," says LeRoy. "At the station."

She just nods. It might be because of the moment, it might be because she is young, but she is not unnerved. Not that LeRoy can tell. He feels sorry for her, he feels as if he has been proved right, and he wishes he didn't have the burden of his knowledge. That this day will not end the way she planned. He grabs her duffel bag, which isn't even full, and it makes him sad to think of the meager start she plans for her life. She carries her school backpack over both her shoulders. She wears her curly hair back in a ponytail. Her youth is unmistakable.

When the door opens behind them, they both instinctively try to ignore it and keep walking to the car.

"Roy, that you, young fellow?" says her father, still swaying slightly from the night before.

LeRoy stops and turns in the little sidewalk that leads to the street. Cleo keeps walking to the car. Her father—a man almost as dark as LeRoy, and thicker, built by a life of work—stands in the doorway with his hands joined on top of his head.

"You been all right, son?" asks her father.

"Yes, sir," says LeRoy. "Store's going good. Even the corporate folks are noticing."

"That's good," says her father. "Boy's got a head for business," he shouts out to Cleo. "What you got a head for?" he asks her, and he laughs and shakes his head. She ignores him, takes her pack off her back and waits, arms folded, for LeRoy. Her father leans in. "You watch her, Roy. Child don't know how to get in from the rain."

"I'm trying, sir."

"What time you coming home?" he shouts out to the street.

"Got a test tonight. Not 'til late." She doesn't look at him.

"You call me when you get off work," he says. "Let me know where you are."

"We better be getting on," says LeRoy.

"Got a show to run, young fellow," says her father. "You got your head on, boy. I tell you, now, watch that little one out there. She's trouble waiting for an excuse."

LeRoy nods, waits until the door is closed before turning to the car. Cleo is staring straight at him, expectant. She looks exactly like a child.

The bus station is downtown, not far. They drive a while before she speaks.

"Thank you for that," she says. "I know you don't want to do this. You could've ended it right there."

He shrugs in response, mainly because the idea almost comes to him as a surprise, that he could've stopped all this. He wants to change the subject but he can't think of anything to say so he just blurts it out.

"He's not coming."

She is looking straight ahead when he says it and she doesn't shift her gaze.

"Why?" is all she says. She doesn't really seem surprised.

"I don't know," says LeRoy. "He just didn't have the stomach for it, I guess." He assumes she will cry, that she will make him turn the car around, that she will make up some lie for her father about why she's home—a scheduling mix-up at the restaurant, extra studying

for her test—and she will sleep fitfully through most of the rest of
the day. But she doesn't do any of that.

"Do you think they'll refund the extra ticket?" She turns, finally,
to look at him when she asks this, an honest, earnest question.

"You can't go," he says at first. When she doesn't respond, he says,
"You got nothing—not even clothes enough to fill up two bags."

"Aunt Lucy's in Iowa waiting for me. I'll go there. She'll know
what to do."

What he doesn't ask is why—why she needs to go. Maybe he
knows, maybe he doesn't yet let himself know. Instead, he sees her
father's mouth, the words coming out in slow motion: watch her.

"I'll go, too," he says.

"You can't," she says, and she smiles at him. A real smile, with
love. "You've got a show to run."

He watches her ascending the stairs into the bus and, yes, she
is still like a child, but now it is more than that. She turns halfway
around as she walks and gives him a wave, small but confident, fully
alive, and she disappears.

"I'll let you know how it turns out," she had said to him, waiting
in line to board the bus. He believed her then. Now he has backed
away from her, and he walks to his car. He would've waited until
the bus pulled out, waved her away, but the windows were tinted
and he couldn't see in. He had no way of knowing which seat she
chose, where she was.

When he is halfway to the restaurant, heading irreconcilably away
from her, he comes to realize that he is a stupid, dense man—like
many men—who sees only what he wants to see, only what he's
ready for. He makes a dangerous U-turn on a red light, causing at
least one car to skid towards the median, and he swerves in and out
of traffic, making his way for the highway. He has the vague idea that

he will follow the bus all the way to Dubuque, Des Moines—wherever it carries her, and he will be there for her when she steps off. The traffic is dense, increasing with the day. He believes, somehow, he can undo almost all of it and catch her in time.

Sister Blanche

Day after day, I imagine, the girls come, mostly somber, sometimes angry or with a dumb-luck fatness in their faces. Afternoon sun fills the room. The ones who bring their beaus are the ones who still believe there is a future to be had.

†

Just after Mother died, I toured New England with Cherie, my sister. Neither of us had been to the Northeast and we went for different reasons. I went to see Emily Dickinson's house.

"You've lived her life and you weren't even trying," Cherie told me. We were on the walk in between the two adjacent Dickinson properties, the family house and that of Emily's beloved brother.

"Yes," I said. I said it then because it was something to say. I said it though I knew, coming from Cherie, it was not a compliment.

For her part, Cherie went to New England because she had been told an old beau—now widowed—was there. She did not know where, or how to find him, or even if it was true. The man's name was Bill. Friends of hers said they had heard he might be living on the coast.

"That makes me happy. He adored the water," she said to me. "How lovely."

My sister is a sad woman who does not like to be alone, which makes much of what she says and does transparent to me. All during the early stages of our trip, she could not help but imagine herself arm-in-arm with a paunchier version of the sable-haired boy with whom she had been young thirty years ago. She did not say as much, but I knew it from her eyes and gait and from the things she packed: *How big can New England be?*

†

I know that they are only letters, mostly unsent, and that those I *have* sent have barely caused a ripple in one man's life half a nation away. I think my guilt stems from the fact that I knew it might happen this way even before it did. I did not know for sure that we would find him. In the grand scheme of things, New England is relatively large. I knew, however, that if we found him—I knew if we found him, there was no predicting the outcome. My sister is still an attractive woman in many ways—her skin is smooth, her nose is a button, and her small breasts have made good use of their advantages against gravity. I, on the other hand, have never been pretty, and I am small and stocky, with a ruddy face and short, graying red hair. This—the contrast between my pretty sister and me—is the way it has always been. I am used to the idea. The difference now is that my sister has the look of a woman who has run out of the luck she used to take for granted. I do not have, and have never had, that look.

At any rate: it turned out that Bill lived in the Vermont woods, a good distance from any coast. But because his surname is unusual— Tblisi—and because Cherie can be dogged in her flight from lone-liness, we were able to enlist the help of a very eager librarian at Amherst College to find him.

"You can be found these days," the woman told us. This was not meant to be threatening. It was a reassurance, as was the warm, white glow of a computer monitor beaming off her eyeglasses and her shiny nose.

Cherie feigned something on the order of indifference. If not indifference, then a willingness to be properly deliberate about when we left for Vermont.

"Lunch first," she said. "You look peaked."

"The portions at breakfast were dramatic," I said. "I am still recovering."

"Well, all right then, I guess we might as well make an adventure of it."

So we drove, mostly in silence, through the hills of western Massachusetts, across the border, and into the green land of Vermont. I find it calming when things are aptly named, when something is called directly what it is. Vermont is a "green mountain" and so, as we drove, I basked in the trustworthiness of the place and the people—Frenchmen, I suppose—who named it. It disarmed me and I fell into a sort of trance as the warm sun shone onto my lap in the passenger's seat of our rented car. With the road map spread out before me, I caught myself hoping that upon seeing Cherie again, Bill would grab her, swoop her up and spin her round and round in an emphatic, unmistakable embrace. For just a moment, I was nearly sure I would make the trip home alone, that all of Cherie's life had been but a preparation for this very reunion. I was pleased that this pleased me, and a little surprised.

When we pulled off the interstate and onto an unlined rural route, it was nearly three o'clock and my stomach grumbled. Cherie heard it and tried to ignore it but when it happened again, she fished a pack of mints from her purse and handed it to me.

"How much further?" she said.

"Not far." I sucked on two mints at once and my stomach quieted some.

"Should we phone?" I said.

"Yes," she said. "Of course. It's rude otherwise. We'll find a phone when we get to Bradley."

"Bradford," I corrected.

"Yes," said Cherie. "Bradford."

I waited in the car as Cherie made the call from a filling station. I stared at the side mirror, which was angled down and reflected the gray gravel, stained here and there with oil. I chose not to watch Cherie, who stood at the phone booth several feet in front of the car. I did not want to see the awkward first few seconds of conversation. Bill almost surely would need help remembering her, though there may have been a time when he was familiar enough with the contours of her back and the secrets of her undergarments that he could unclasp her brassiere with just his off hand, kissing her all the while.

"We're not far away at all," she said when she got back in the car. "He sounds just the same. The same Billy Tblisi."

I could tell there was a wish embedded in this assessment. A hope. Yes, the timbre of his voice, his inflections, his polite laugh—all of that must have resembled whatever versions of him she could dredge up in her memory. But there is no way of telling if someone has made a disaster of the last thirty years until you see him from a few feet away, maybe not even until you hold him in your arms.

†

On the face of things, William E. Tblisi, M.D., had never known failure. He left Cherie and the rest of our insular province behind when he went north to attend Mr. Jefferson's college in Virginia. Next was Yale for medicine, followed by a residency in pulmonology at a prestigious hospital in New York. There, he met a Belgian woman, Monique, who had been an impossibly leggy runway model—Milan, Paris, New York—until a mysterious wheeze evolved into a debilitating shortness of breath, then an unseemly chronic hack, which in turn led Monique to the young Dr. Tblisi's office. It was a matter of months and they were married—and happily so for two decades until her weak lungs gave in and Billy Tblisi became the widower he was destined to be.

The last two years of Monique's life were spent in the Vermont woods, away from the city and its smog, in a house her doting husband built especially for her. It was the house he still occupied, tucked back three-quarters of a mile off the main road, under a green canopy, the very house Cherie and I drove up to that day this past spring. The large structure climbed three stories into the clean sky. It was not shaped like an ordinary house. Where angles and flatness and siding would normally be, there were smooth-arcing walls of dark wood and pleasant little curved alcoves. It had the air of sculpture. In the two-acre clearing, dotted with wildflowers, there was a large outcropping of granite that dipped into the shape of a bowl, pooling a clear sheen of rainwater. A tiered garden—vegetables, exotic-looking herbs—bordered the far edge of the forest.

"Oh," Cherie managed. There was not much more to do but gasp quietly at the Eden he had made. Before our car poked to the end of the drive, Bill Tblisi emerged from the house. He waved in a quick, familiar gesture, as if he had been expecting us for ages. Bill wore a plain blue t-shirt, chinos rolled casually at the cuff, and European sandals. Underneath a well-worn Boston Red Sox cap spilled a considerable amount of brilliant, prematurely white hair. He was handsomer than I expected him to be, and trimmer. I think all of that made Cherie oddly disheartened because, as a reflex, she criticized him under her breath—"Somebody thinks he's still a little boy, I see." But she gathered herself and beamed the smile she had cultivated from the time, as a mere girl, she realized it was something she could wield.

"Dr. Tblisi, I presume," she joked through the car's open window. He laughed appropriately as he walked toward us. There were, of course, hugs—even one for me, though I am sure he did not remember me from so long ago; we had only met twice or maybe three times. I cannot speak for Cherie, but the man I held for that small moment was anything but a disaster. He was sure, in every still-firm muscle, and though he was somewhat short of stature and Mother always told us that short men often overseek to make up for their lack of height, Bill Tblisi was a peaceful man at home within himself.

"I hope you girls will stay for dinner," he said right away. "I've got a ton of snap beans. Red and green peppers too. I have to do something with them or else they'll go to waste."

Stay for dinner (pasta primavera, tart chardonnay, crusty bread, melon slices with prosciutto for dessert) we did. All told, we stayed for six more dinners, in fact, and all the other meals in between. When Bill heard that our tour was rather aimless and that we did not have much to press us back home, he insisted that we stay with him as long as we liked. The company, he said, was a very pleasant novelty.

"I kept telling Monique we needed some children," he joked. "Else retirement would be boring as hell."

"And what did she say to that?" Cherie's voice carried just a tinge of reproach for the dead model, a tinge made more discernible by a late-afternoon, white-wine buzz.

"She just grabbed me from behind and kissed me on the ear and told me she couldn't share me with anybody, not even her own babies."

Because I know my sister, I know quite well that this disgusted her. She has never been one for saccharine reminiscences of the dearly departed. Not after her own husband, Martin, died slowly and painfully of bone cancer. Certainly not after Mother. But in this case, on Billy Tblisi's perfect deck, on the fringe of his perfect house and life, she simply patted his hand and, without asking, got up to fetch the bottle of wine from the kitchen to refill our glasses.

Bill and I sat and listened to the strange northeastern birds.

"Actually" he said. "I like that there's nothing to say or do. As long as every once in a while there's somebody around to do it with."

†

The time came when even the most obtuse houseguest would know to leave, even in the face of great protest from his host. We had wandered far afield in New England: camped one night in the White Mountains, ate ice cream on the shores of Lake Champlain, daytripped to Boston, tramped around Walden Pond, and so on. I think Cherie was not above waiting for some kind of proposal, formal or not, and she would have even settled for including me in the bargain. But when it became clear that, while we could stay indefinitely, we would always be guests from far off, she decided it was time to pull away—if for no other reason than a shift in strategy. She hugged him tight and spoke straight into his ear the morning we drove to the airport.

"Please, Bill," she told him, "use that telephone you've got. Thirty years more and we'll all be dead."

I had already hugged him. Afterwards he had pecked me on the cheek and handed me a note with his address on it. "I love to get letters," he told us, though he was only looking at me. After her hug, Cherie jutted out her cheek and, after an imperceptible pause, Bill followed suit with a kiss for her as well.

When we were taxiing down the runway, Cherie turned to me and said, "I don't think he was even going to kiss me on the cheek. He kissed you and I think he thought that covered it."

"You think too much. If I were you, I would think less about such things."

"But you're not me," she said. "We know that."

"And so does Bill."

"What does that mean?" she said. "Blanche? What could you possibly mean by that?"

I said I meant nothing by it, absolutely nothing, and then I turned my head to look out the window as the huge metal craft tugged ever higher into the air.

†

It might have been the fact that, in the midst of a long and often difficult hike one warm afternoon, I waded out on the slippery rocks by myself and floated on my back in a still-icy stream adjacent to our path. Maybe it was because I rarely spoke and he could make me into whatever he wanted me to be. Really, there is no telling the specific reason. I think, generally, it happened because I am not my sister, and specifically it happened because I do not say much. Some things do not need more explanation than that.

At any rate, Bill Tblisi wrote me in short order after our trip. He replied to my sweet, pithy thank-you note with four-and-a-half pages on good paper in a tight, neat hand. There were no heartfelt confessions, nor did I expect any. His missive simply contained news of the day, but there was something about it—maybe its sheer length—that suggested he had not sent another like it to Cherie. When I inquired, obliquely, whether she had heard from him yet, I could hear her stifle a sigh on the other end of the telephone.

"It's not his way," she said. "Perhaps I should call him."

I told her that, yes, perhaps she should. In fact, I think I was fairly encouraging about it because by the end of the conversation, Cherie was giddy as a schoolgirl.

"Do you *really* think I should call him? Just call him?" she said. "I wouldn't want to wreck his peace and quiet. What if he thinks I'm after him?"

"You are after him," I said.

"Oh, Blanche, don't be crude."

Like the aforementioned schoolgirl, Cherie wrung her hands for weeks about whether or not to phone Bill Tblisi. In the meantime, I had replied to his first letter with a letter of my own—in ballpoint pen on college-ruled paper: I avoid slanting lines if I can help it. I mainly responded to what he had written: my time, I wrote, was largely occupied with morning walks, afternoon walks, cups of coffee and tea, reading, light lunches and suppers. I told him I was thinking of getting a dog or a bird, which was true, something to tend to. I told him that while others might think a middle age of idleness—of mere puttering, sipping things, reading, listening to the insects sing in the summer—was a slow burn to insanity, it was mostly fine with me. What I did not tell him was that I had aspired to this life for quite some time, that, upon Mother's death, my mind went immediately to calculations, the power of a largish inheritance to grow of its own accord. The dirt over her casket had not yet settled before I turned in my notice to the head curator at the natural history museum, where I had been his top assistant for seventeen years. I did not tell Bill Tblisi that my relative happiness and contentment was the net result of my mother's death.

He wrote back quickly, on the same brand of paper, in the same hand. This time he wrote about his own idleness.

> I knew I would end up here. That was the hard part about life with Monique. As a doctor, I knew how long we had left. This house was partly for her, to give her a peaceful last few years away from everything. But we always knew that this is where I would die too. And that there would be a long pyrrhic season of widowerhood. She knew it better than me. And I'm healthy as a goddamned horse. Sometimes I feel like an exile, like I'm waiting a very long time to die, but there is nowhere else I want to be and I've done most of what I want to do. I guess I know I'm happy where I am because I know for sure I wouldn't be happy anywhere else. Is this something you have felt? It would be nice to know I'm not alone in this. Yes, I'm aware of the irony in that statement. I do like to be alone most of the time.

I was sure that Bill was not writing the letters entirely for me. My name and address went on the envelope, of course, and he was appropriately warm and personal towards me. Even attentive. But they were letters from the other side of something, from a place where only he could be. I imagine he chose me as a correspondent because he saw something of that in me during our short visit. For some reason—maybe that one—I found it more and more difficult to reply. I wrote—volumes; it was not that I did not write. I simply let the letters—signed and sealed and some even stamped—pile up in the desk drawer. To keep him writing, I sent a note, here and there—the equivalent of a sympathetic nod in conversation.

†

Shortly after my correspondence with Bill began in earnest, I started to change my afternoon walking route. I live in an eclectic section of the city—there are garden apartments, million-dollar homes, the Christian Science Reading Room, a retirement community. Tattooed young men glide here and there on skateboards. Four blocks down is a housing project. There are temples and mosques, and gay men troll for one another in the city park adjacent to a large, stony Methodist church. Which is to say, a turn here or there can lead to any of a number of different worlds.

For several months after Mother's death, I traveled the same route up the crest, higher and higher, into the opulent neighborhoods. I walked this way because it led to the most spectacular view of the city. When I reached the summit, I could walk along a row of Italianate mansions on my left, with the wide expanse of the city and the horizon, sweeping and panoramic, on my right. I was accustomed to my route—the steep up-and-down-and-up that made my heart throb at intervals; the blind spots where sleek luxury vehicles might careen around a curve and come menacingly close to the walk; how the restless sun changed the trees and their shadows over the course of a day. All of it was a comfort to me and comfort, before Bill's letters, was something I aimed for, at the exclusion of all else.

Anticipating the postman is not a comfortable pastime, though. Nor is spending most of every afternoon and evening writing expansive letters that are not likely to be sent. Certainly keeping all of that from one's closest living relative—one with an abiding, vested interest in the matter—can be discomfiting as well. But as the level of my psychic unease rose, so—strangely—did my tolerance (even appetite) for it. I began to wrest myself away from certain patterns in my life, patterns I had previously thought were sustaining me. It was, for instance, my habit to phone Cherie every morning at ten, after my coffee but before my daily shower. Then, much to my surprise, I received a call from her one morning around that time.

"Blanche?" she said. "For heaven's sake, I thought I was going to have to get someone to bust down your door. It's been three days since I've heard from you."

I lied—another thing I ordinarily never do—and told her that the curator had called: three of his four docents *and* my replacement had all come down with the walking pneumonia (or some such) and he begged for my help in setting up an enormous new exhibit that was already behind schedule. I was, I told her, just too exhausted to keep track of anything else for the last few days. She believed me, of course, because nothing so unusual had ever happened to me before and because, as far as Cherie was concerned, there would be no reason for me to lie. Besides, Cherie had finally screwed up the nerve to call Bill and she wanted to run her plan by me. As long as I was alive, unbound, ungagged, inviolate, she felt safe to proceed to more urgent concerns.

"I think," she schemed, "it's best not to mention the fact that he hasn't called. Don't you?"

I told her I thought that was best.

"Because he *knows* he hasn't called, and if he hasn't called because he just doesn't care to talk to me, well, it doesn't exactly do me any good to point that out."

"He'll be happy to talk to you."

"Do you think so, Blanche? I hope you're right. I think I miss him."

I stifled a snort. I knew that she did not miss Bill Tblisi. Even I did not miss Bill Tblisi. Not really. Bill Tblisi was not the sort of person who wanted to be missed.

†

It is possible or even likely that, on some level, Cherie grew wise to my inchoate connection to Bill Tblisi. Not precisely—not the minutiae. And not, of course, that anything was going to come of it—not in the sense that would have horrified her most. That is to say, William Tblisi and I were not deep in negotiation to merge our interests; I was not—nor would I ever be—headed to live out my days in his fabricated Eden. As long as this was not the outcome, Cherie knew as much as she wanted to know from the phone call she finally made. It took her several more days—graphing out the trajectory of what such a conversation might turn out to be, jotting notes, talking points. She had decided on a ruse—that she had begun a garden and wanted advice. She thought the subtle symbolism was fitting. I told her I thought so too. But, alas, as most fretted-over conversations go, this one was uneventful, mundane. It lasted six and a half minutes.

"What else did he say?" I asked.

"I don't remember," she said. "There was nothing to it."

"He had to say something," I said. "Niceties, at least."

"Of course," Cherie said. She was matter-of-fact. Bored, even. And then this: "He said he's been writing lots of letters lately."

"Really? To whom?"

"Friends. I don't really know."

"Did he offer to write you?" I said.

"I told him letters were so distant and slow and that as I get older they make me feel like I'm running out of time."

"What did he say to that?"

"He said all he has is time. God, Blanche," she said, "he reminds me of you."

I didn't say anything. I came to realize I was holding my breath.

"Not that there's anything wrong with that," she said. "Just that I've already got a Blanche in my life. I don't need another one."

I forced a laugh at her halfway joke, mumbled something about my walk, and hurried off the phone.

✝

My walk that afternoon was more a foray than it was a walk. I turned down streets I had barely paid attention to before then. One led me to a small park where a single, solitary man, gaunt in a sleeveless shirt, strutted around, snapping his arrhythmic fingers to "Killing Me Softly," which blared from the portable radio he had set in the grass. I watched him strike poses, unconcerned and oblivious. Up the road from the park I walked past two myna birds perched on a rusted lawnmower, c. 1952, in someone's otherwise pristine front lawn. They clicked their massive beaks so that the sound echoed through the quiet neighborhood. While the noise lingered, the place had the air of a jungle. As if it was wild. Then the quiet settled back in, punctured only once by the distant diesel-chug of a Mercedes climbing the hill. Down and to the right three blocks, I came to a small parochial school—St. Rose of Lima—with its alabaster Christ, risen, arms outstretched, in the middle of an unremarkable court-yard. Normally I do not stop my walks under any circumstances, but in this case I did. I made my way to the very center of the courtyard and gave myself an audience with the Prince of Peace. His arms were spread to me. His lips were locked. There was no noise whatsoever as the heat of the day built upon itself.

From there, I continued down Arlington Crescent, winding back in through the quiet, tree-lined neighborhood. Almost as if I had been seeking it, the clinic presented itself to me for the first time. I had not known it was so close to my apartment, ensconced several yards from the street in a refurbished, red brick building that may have once housed a family. As soon as I saw the sign, understated but forceful, citing a litany of federal laws mandating the exact mini-mum distance between protesters and clientele, I felt a faint but unmistakable phantom sympathy in my groin. I thought, perhaps for obvious reasons, of my mother, who famously did not believe in such pains—if it did not bleed or swell or throb, it did not exist.

I think this was because real pain meant so much to her. She used to tell Cherie and me that the highlight of her then-young life was gazing down into the stupid, blank eyes of her babies just after we had been born, just after we had ripped ourselves out of her. There was no mistaking the source of her joy, this joy burned straight through her. She bled from it. That is the way she said it to us, even as children. Unadorned. We were to take from it only exactly what she meant: The very first sensation she felt on our account was an excruciating, nauseating, unforgettable hurt.

†

I now find myself where I always do at this time of day. Soon, the tea kettle will hum, then sing, on the burner. My evening will step in line, follow suit with all the other evenings. I will sip tea and find a quiet way to fill the few hours before bed. I sit at the desk, pondering a drawer full of letters unsent. I am now prepared to burn them, to purge even the possibility that they might set forth into the world and find a communicative purchase. What, after all, would it change for someone else—someone far away and alien to my day-to-day living—to have a record of my inner thoughts? I do not miss Bill Tblisi. I do not even know him. The letters in the drawer are not meant for him, just as his are never really meant for me.

I tread into the kitchen—I am still wearing the orthopedic sneakers from my walk—to find the large stainless steel pot in which I ordinarily boil cabbage, whole chickens. A utensil big enough for all-day simmers. There are matches in the utility drawer, and I grab those too. Back at my desk, I pull the drawer out and dump the letters and whatever else it contains into the big pot. As I strike the match, I worry that the fire I am about to start will never stop burning. But there is less flame than I imagined, and the burning is slow. The flimsy paper of an old receipt gives itself up quickly, but the stuffed envelopes are heartier. They blacken and glow at the edges. The slow flame trudges along from one letter to another, almost reluctant, and then it dies.

I start to light another match, then stop. Ordinarily I am not one to change my mind. My constancy is a source of pride. But it occurs to me there is only one thing to do with these singed letters. Especially *because* they are now singed. I reach down to pick up the pot full of smoldering paper. I expect the handles to be warm but they are not. As I walk out the door, the kettle starts its shrill singing, but I do not stop or put the pot down. I take the steps two at a time and my walk is brisk, purposeful. The sun is cooling and just about to hide behind the retirement community for the night. I scan my neighborhood quickly, looking for the familiar, squat blue postal bin. Because they are everywhere and rarely useful, they blend into the scenery, stealthy as spies. There is one at the end of my block. I am sure I have never seen it there before. When I reach it, I open the heavy lid and pour what is in the pot down its silent, waiting throat.

†

The way back up the block to my apartment is slower, more contemplative, more like me. Some of the letters were never stamped. The integrity of several envelopes has been compromised by the fire. Half or more of them will never come close to where they were meant to go. But some of them—a few at least—will. I feel sure I have now sent enough of me into the world to last my remaining days. I imagine the sheer volume of words—words on top of words on top of words—will be enough to keep Billy Tblisi from ever writing me again. Just now, as if for the first time, I am aware of an unavoidable and comforting truth about the world. Most things do not take root, and that is as it was intended. Surer of this with each step, I allow the silver pot to swing lightly in my hand. Ascending the front steps, now almost fully restored, I hear my kettle's angry song.

Resident

On windy days, Esterowicz harkens back to his youth, on the plains, in the flat midriff of this country. There, the air was impeded only by grass and clouds. It came in straight and relentless. He spent long afternoons as a child, alone, out in the fields, flying the kites his uncles made and repaired for a hobby. They were glad for him because they had long outgrown the need to fly the kites themselves; they were only still attached to the making. The thrill of finding more-adhesive glues, stronger papers, the delight in lighter and lighter kinds of wood. Esterowicz was the only person in his family who ran with the kites trailing above and behind, darting madly through the air. Now, in his apartment, hundreds of miles south and east, dozens of years later, Esterowicz contemplates this windy day in February. It is the only day off he will have for two weeks. There is a pile of aqua scrubs in the corner and a mattress on the floor and the carcass of a wasp on the windowsill. Dishes in the sink. A moist towel on the rack in the bathroom. That's it. The sum of his existence outside his vocation. Each day, he ventures downtown, into the small, smoky city, to understand the things that make a body work, that undermine it. He has come here to do that and only that, and when he is done with his studies, he will leave, go back to Chicago, forget most of what he did here in his rare free time. Mostly he will recall how this place is buffered against great winds by the small ridge that runs across its flank. In February, though, the wind gets wily. It gathers, circles into long columns, spins down valleys and over foothills. It *does* sound like a freight train. It *does* lift houses whole, deposit them miles away. Esterowicz stares out the window, sipping at a cup of tea with too much honey, lusting after the hellacious dipsy-doodles such a wind might conceive.

Hereafter

Yvonne's fat child, Robert, licked his fingers. His stubby legs dangled from the buggy. Orange Icee dripped down his equally stubby forearm in a long, cold, neon-colored tear. Yvonne kept her eyes ahead, looking past the child and to the right, perusing the dried beans, the half-a-dozen kinds of rice her upscale grocery offered. Basmati. Short-grain brown. Long-grain brown. Converted. Jasmine. Wild.

"Mother," Robert asked—his face had been screwed into a perpetual grimace since the moment he slid from her womb, "when am I going to die?"

This was the third time he had asked her the question that day, and he had asked it dozens of times in the three days since they had buried her father. She answered it as she had been doing.

"When you're 84, Robby," she muttered. "You've still got seventy-six more years to go. That's a long time."

"I don't believe you," he said. "How do you know?"

The truth was, she didn't know. The only thing she knew these days was that she didn't know much. Her father had been fifty-four when he'd had his first open-heart surgery. He was fifty-five when he had the second, and then six years after that, they cut a hole through his throat to remove his cancerous larynx. Less than a year later— after his doctor declared him cancer-free, invincible, nothing less than an inspiration—a blood clot popped behind his right eye, leaving him to spend his last few days on earth paralyzed on one side, pissing and shitting himself, surrounded by people who were now strangers to him. He had shouted at them—if his garbled, hoarse whisper still counted as shouting—to let him watch the goddamn Arnold Schwarzenegger movie in one fucking minute of peace. But there was no Schwarzenegger movie, not even a television. His last, labored effort at communication was to let them know he had to pee. Yvonne's son was asking her to make sense of a world where this could be a good man's final course.

All she had to offer the boy was a feeble, "I just know."

Yvonne had long fled from any sign of her age. Snips here, lifts there, two separate breast augmentations—one to firm things up after Robert's arrival, and another last December just because. It wasn't that she wanted for the attention of men. She had it, even her husband's. It was that her life—motherhood especially—caused her to feel as if all the world, *everything*, was happening somewhere else. When she was in her twenties, the idea of a child or even a husband sent a decided shiver through the insides of her. She loved her life of shortish skirts and longish heels and social cigarettes, the small but pervasive concerns of a career in marketing. She loved even more the consistent shelf life associated with serial monogamy—the security in knowing all relationships had a beginning, a middle, and a certifiable, like-clockwork end. But somehow all that became passé. She wasn't sure when or how. It seemed that overnight, her compatriots at all her favorite bars were five years younger than she was; everyone her age was married and chafing themselves to distraction in a perfunctory effort to turn a tangled knot of DNA into a living, breathing, defecating thing.

Then Bob came along—the deluxe version of all the men she had been dating: solid, strong, straight-toothed, eager. An ophthalmologist by trade and temperament, he didn't so much sweep her off her feet as help her see very clearly that their union was the natural chain of events: a wedding with too many guests, merged 401(k)s with too many overlapping mutual funds, a dog with too much hair, and a house with more bathrooms, backyard, and closet space than they needed. Soon enough, that chain also included Robert. Too much of him from the very beginning had necessitated the first breast surgery and a tummy tuck, not to mention the episiotomy that took twice as long as it should have to heal.

The idea had been that she would work part-time from home until Robert went to school, but he had just finished kindergarten and things didn't seem to be working out that way. One thing conspired with another and inertia had set in. Her career was a fallow field. Still, she clung to the idea that one day she might go back to it full-time and she wanted to look not a day older than when she had stopped. She ran five times a week, ate just a touch less than she should have, and supplemented with all manner of herbs, vitamins, and minerals. A fresh bottle of purified water was never very far from her lips. There were cucumber masks and hypoallergenic lotions, regular appointments with acupuncturists, rolfing specialists, yoga instructors, meditation gurus. The most obvious result of all this was that Yvonne—always a comely woman—looked just about like a movie star, prettier and more alive than she ever had. Only upon very close inspection might someone search out a stray crow's foot, the infinitesimal tributary of a laugh line.

Eggplant. Fresh basil, arugula. Kale. Chard. Pomegranate juice. A package of prunes touting their unmatched antioxidant virtues: *16 x more Vitamin A than bananas! 8 x more potassium than apples; 6 x more B vitamins than oranges!* Despite their nutritional inferiority, there were bananas, apples, and oranges in the buggy as well. There was also a large package of bologna with a red plastic rind, a monstrous block of Velveeta.

These and other items like it—food she kept in the house only grudg-
ingly because the boy wouldn't eat anything else—she separated
from the less processed foods—her foods, so that it appeared as if
she was shopping for two separate households. Robert grabbed for a
giant bag of potato chips, but Yvonne swerved the buggy so that his
little arms couldn't reach.

"I've told you three times—no more chips until you finish the
open bags we have at home."

"They're all smushed," he said, grimacing still. "I only like it
when the chips are whole chips."

Yvonne kept going and didn't address him, so he shrieked. "I
want new chips!" It was when she looked away from her son's beet-
red face, his sticky and wide-open mouth, that she noticed the man
staring at her from the end of the aisle. He was scruffy-just-so and
young and decked out in medical scrubs. When he saw that Yvonne
noticed him noticing her, his mouth curved into a tiny smile and he
turned his attention back to the pretzels. Robert was still at full wail
as they passed the man.

"Hush, Robert," she told him. "People are trying to get their
groceries in peace."

"I don't care," the boy screamed. "Not even a little!" Or that is
what he intended to say, but the words were garbled and, at best,
he spat them out halfway formed. Yvonne caught the young man's
eye again and he smiled again, this time as a gesture of sympathy.

"I'm sorry," she said. "I can't take him anywhere."

"Occupational hazard," he said.

"You don't know the half of it," she said, and she laughed in the
way strangers laugh for each other.

Yvonne's mind fingered through what the rest of the day promised.
In the immediate future, there would be the long conveyor belt of

the checkout line, an equally long receipt and a three-figure debit from the checking account that bore her husband's name as the principal account holder. She would pile the plastic bags—some heavy, laden with cold perishables, others light with one or two dry items—into the trunk of her well-engineered minivan. Then she would strap her restless son into the backseat, and drive the 6.7 miles to her suburban manse, where she would lug the bags in and get started on the long, slow chore of putting the groceries away. There would be the problem of getting Robert his snack and parking him in front of the TV, the sounds of explosions and roars and the shouts of strong, outsized cartoon-men filling the family room. When that got to be too much for her, she would cajole him to go outside, to stretch his legs at the very least, otherwise he would never sleep later that evening. Then, in the period of time before sundown, when Robert was gone and she was alone in the house, she would finish with the rest of the groceries, plan dinner, and then blanche or marinate or otherwise prepare whatever needed it. Still, in the face of all this doing—this mothering, this planning and organizing and putting away, this chopping and dicing and pouring and measuring—there would almost always be a period of several long minutes when there was nothing to do but sit and wait. She dreaded it the most.

As a way to postpone the inevitable, Yvonne tooled aimlessly around the grocery store. Robert's screaming had subsided into an occasional whimper and some huffy breathing. The buggy was becoming heavy and difficult to maneuver. It had been several minutes since it had reached the perfect weight—the point at which she could feel that she had done enough shopping for the time being. Still, she tooled. Up and down aisles packed with items she didn't intend to buy. She maintained the proper ratio of head swiveling, so as to appear to the naked eye as if she was searching for something.

"Mother," Robert finally said. "Let's go."

"Honey, I'm looking for something."

"We have everything. Let's go home. I'm hungry."

"I feel like I'm forgetting something," Yvonne said, still searching the aisles. "I'll know it when I see it. Just be patient for a little while longer."

Soon enough, in the frozen foods section, they happened again upon the young man in scrubs.

"We meet again," he said. The smile came easily to his face.

What kind of man is this? Yvonne thought. *I'm ten years older than him. I am pushing a squirmy child in a buggy.* She returned the smile and tucked her hair behind her ear by some vestigial instinct. The man turned his attention to Robert.

"You making life hard for dear old mom?" he asked. Yvonne noticed the adjective. Old. Robert looked down and away from the man and, as he sometimes did in times of stress, grabbed hold of his crotch with both hands.

"I think it's the Y-chromosome," said Yvonne, who tried to tug the boy's fists from his private place as inconspicuously as she could. "Either that or karma."

"Are they mutually exclusive?" said the man. "Maybe just the opposite." Yvonne did not know what he meant by that, exactly, but it didn't really matter. Her heart beat a little faster. She had risked disparaging her son—and, by extension, men in general—and then herself, but the stranger had returned the volley.

This could lead nowhere. She knew that.

Yvonne tucked some hair behind her other ear. Robert pulled at his crotch.

A conversation began in earnest. He was a resident at the downtown university hospital. He was from Chicago. He still had time before he had to decide his specialty. Oncology. Obstetrics. (*As long as it starts in O,* he joked.) He did not have a reason to know her husband but he did work with a friend of a friend. His eyes were a deep, solid brown. His lashes were just a little bit longer than normal. Yvonne thought of Bob, how in the last few years he had begun to grow slight, wispy excesses of hair in undesirable places. The very tops and bottoms of his ears. His shoulder blades. This young man—he was, like Bob, a very handsome man—did not have any of that. But he would. Where and when were the only questions. Like Bob, he would somehow be the better for it. His presence larger, stronger. As if this unwanted hair was evidence of him growing into himself. As if youth was the only thing holding him back. She thought all of these things as they talked for several more minutes. Twice she gave him overt chances to duck out of the conversation. Twice he refused them. *He's lonely*, she thought. *He does nothing but work and go home so he can sleep and work some more.* She watched his lips move but the sound blurred as she imagined what would happen if she invited him to dinner. That night, even. He could follow her home. She could assign him helpful kitchen tasks and then, when there were lulls while something marinated or soaked, they could sip overfull glasses of chardonnay, listen to Robert's cartoon white noise waft in from the other room, and wait, together, for her husband to come home. Nothing more and nothing less than that. She began to consider the question of how Bob would react to a stranger sipping wine in his kitchen, with his wife. More accurately, she was trying to decide how she felt about the fact that Bob would most likely just pour himself a glass and start trading interminable medical community gossip. Who played poker with whom. The scourge of malpractice insurance. Mid-life crises that seemed to start earlier and earlier.

"Mom," came the little voice behind her.

"Just a second, Robert, I'm having a conversation."

"Mommy," repeated Robert.

"I said..." started Yvonne, but she stopped when she noticed the resident's eyes widening. She turned to see an expanding dark splotch creeping down the inside of Robert's shorts. Several hearty, pungent streams of urine dribbled over his bare legs and onto the floor.

"Robert!" she shouted. "Oh my god—"

At her tone, Robert's face crumpled into a full bawl: an unnatural shade of red; gaping mouth; a throaty howl. The resident shuffled nervously at first and then managed to hustle off, presumably in search of someone with a mop and some disinfectant.

As the mother of a six-year-old, Yvonne knew the protocol. She should wait for the unlucky store employee to arrive, apologize profusely, offer to mop the mess herself (this would be refused), and then head off to the bathroom with Robert. But right then, this approach seemed too much like an admission of guilt. No. She would not wait. She would leave, right away.

Only for a brief instant did she contemplate leaving Robert to fend for himself in the buggy, wailing. Instead, she quickly came to her senses and scooped him up—he was so heavy now, it was all she could do to get his legs over the cart—and bolted for the door, leaving all of the groceries behind. She jogged down the aisle and past the check-out lanes, Robert's urine-soaked legs slapping against her hip and backside. She did not stop running until she got to her car, where she plopped her son down in his car seat. As he sniffled and sobbed, she deftly unfastened his shorts and, in one motion, pulled them off along with his soaked underpants. She searched the parking lot for a trashcan, but it was too far away so she tossed the wet clothes onto the front passenger-side floorboard.

"I'm wet," he sobbed.

"I know," said Yvonne, and she slid the door closed. She got in the van, put it in gear, and made a direct line across the nearly empty parking lot to the trashcan. Nearby, an ice-blue Delta 88 inched through the parking lot like a glacier. Even though Yvonne was nowhere near her, the old woman driving the huge car laid on her horn when she saw the van disregard the lanes and zoom across the lot. Yvonne glanced in the mirror at her son whose sobbing had subsided into a generalized expression of fear. She noticed that she had forgotten to buckle him in.

"I'm so hungry," cried Robert. "What about our groceries? Will they bring them to our house?"

Yvonne didn't say anything as the van glided to a halt near the trashcan. With the van still running, she grabbed the soiled clothes and got out. Flies buzzed around the trashcan. The smell was fecal. She turned her head and tossed the shorts into the can, wiping her hand on her shirt. Yvonne circled behind the van and slid open the side door. Her son was quiet, even curious now. She leaned into him, fastening his seat belt, being careful so the belt would not chafe his bare, clammy nether regions.

"Mommy," he said. "I'm hungry."

"I know you are, baby. We'll get you some French fries or something on the way home."

Despite herself, she looked toward the grocery store. She could never go back. Not now, not ever. In the distance, she saw the blue-scrubbed man emerge from the automatic doors. He held one small plastic bag by the handles. He now wore aviator sunglasses and, even so far away, he looked rock solid and beautiful. Yvonne did not know if she wanted him to look for her or not. Either way, he did not. He kept his eyes front, like a soldier, until he reached his sensible mid-sized Japanese car and drove away.

"What are we having for dinner?" asked Robert. He was calm now. It was as if nothing had happened.

"I don't know," she said.

Maybe nothing *had* happened.

Yes. It was true. Everything was the same as it had always been.

Sangha

Roger—the neophyte Zen Buddhist next door—will soon be shot once in the clavicle at close range. His estranged lover, Phillip, will be the shooter. "In a former life, I was an ethnobotanist," Phillip is fond of saying at parties, and it is partway true. Former lives aside, he is now a corporate attorney specializing in pharmaceutical patents. Phillip is tall and rock-jawed and wealthy. His hair is black and wavy and always in place. Phillip—who once ate the brains and spinal tissue of monkeys in a South American jungle as an initiation rite. Phillip—whose mother still calls him *Faggot* to his face. Phillip—who refuses to kiss even Roger on the mouth. This is their downfall.

†

Mariah, upstairs, waxes her lip and thinks of the people she might phone. There is John, the handsome asshole who pays for everything, kisses well enough, and always, maddeningly, climaxes ten seconds too quickly. She decides, once and for all, or at least for now, that John is a frustration beyond measure. She could call her mother, Rosa, who everyone says looks young enough to be her sister. But there is Roger, downstairs, with whom she sometimes sleeps—just sleeps—when she needs a man's warmth and smell for reassurance that there are, indeed, certain things she can count on. Roger's thin frame spoons nicely behind hers. He smells like tobacco and soap and pungent cooking and he wants absolutely nothing from her.

†

Across the hall, Ryan replays his band's afternoon rehearsal. Should Billy and Ryan both sing "yeah, yeah" before the chorus of "Labor of Love," or should it just be a subtle "uh-huh," sung by Ryan's little brother, Matt, the drummer? Maybe the song should instead be called "Love's Labor Lost." Yes. Fuck it. Rush had a literary bent and it didn't really hurt them. But is the world ready for a return to concept albums, that's the real question. Roger would know. Roger, thinks Ryan, knows a lot.

†

Phillip's car—black and German—turns left onto Clairmont Avenue. He flips on his wipers in the face of a fledgling mist. The Piggly Wiggly is lit up to absurd proportions at this time of night. Roger's is two blocks away. Phillip has the gun in his lap, a bullet—just one—in his right breast pocket. As he blinks at the grocery store's ambient light and calms himself to the rhythmic, soft flailing of the wipers, Phillip thinks primarily of Roger's beautiful round head. Some nights, as Roger sat sipping his tea and looking out the window at the shabby apartments across the street, Phillip would hold Roger's stubbled head lightly in both hands, like a globe. Energy would run through his hands. This, he always thought, is what God must have felt like. On the second day.

†

Then there is Adele, who takes pills. She is down the hall from Mariah, directly above Roger, color-coding. It is a medicinal rainbow. Once, after chewing down several primaries—reds, yellows, blues—she found herself in the street, arms spread wide, a dumb grin crawling across her face. She was not wearing any pants. This caused a stir. Hoots, hollers. Roger came to her, wrapped her in a blanket, and called her sister in Atlanta, just as he had done before—time and time again—when things like this happened. Whenever she passed him in the hall or on the way to the mailbox, they barely spoke. Instead, one invariably reached toward the other, and, seeing this—expecting it—the other did the same, until they touched hands lightly, quickly, and went on about their respective ways.

†

Phillip pulls in behind Roger's car—an eight-year-old Nissan with three hubcaps and a bent antenna. As he rests his head on his steering wheel, all he can think about is their one sexual foray in that very vehicle. It had been daring. A whim. They parked under a streetlamp near Rushton Park on Highland Avenue. Roger scooted over to the passenger seat and Phillip hunched down, between his legs, in the well. They made absolutely no noise. Roger was small—no bigger than a fat, stiff index finger—and this was one of the things Phillip loved about his lover. The messes he did not require.

Phillip takes the bullet from his breast pocket and puts it in the chamber. He spins it, as he has seen in movies. He shoves the long barrel all the way down his throat and pulls the trigger. There is a click. He is alive. He succumbs, then, to a string of autonomic dry heaves.

†

Mariah dials and waits. "Maha-Roger," she says into the answering machine, "pick up. Get off that damn meditation mat and join the fucked-up world. The beautiful Mariah has chosen you as her evening's entertainment. The implication, my dear yogi, is that your mere presence is infinitely better than holding a live penis in my hand. Roger, come on. I'm bored." Finally she gives in. She hangs up and goes into the kitchen to pour another glass of wine. She sighs with all of the rest of the fucked-up world.

†

Ryan's hand is on the knob when he is waylaid by the muse:

> No, little angel,
> I'm not your silver cloud
>
> Park your ass somewhere else
> I play my music loud.

He scrambles for the pencil with the little, furry-headed baby-man impaled where the eraser used to be. He scribbles these and other subsequent lyrics—heaven-sent—onto a yellowed receipt for chips, deodorant, milk, and something else. For the time being, he forgets Roger, forgets everything else in the manifest, fucked-up world.

†

Adele's apartment is lit only by the TV. The volume is turned all the way down—Chuck Woolery laughs at a chunky black woman's account of a date with an audience-selected cad. Adele has long since foregone the need for water to wash down the pills. She picks them up from the even, Technicolor sheet they form on the metal TV tray. She eats them one at a time, like Pez candy, staring into Chuck's warm, easy, muted smile.

†

Up the slight slope of the hill, one foot in front of the other along the cracked sidewalk, Phillip makes a slow ascent. One small step up into the courtyard, then fifty feet or so of walkway into the mouth of the building. On either side of him, the building hunkers in, some of the windows open, light and music spilling out, some closed, dark, and quiet. Above that is sky: cloudy, dark, heavy, tinted orange from the city-glow. Phillip walks slowly to the steps leading into the building, his right hand holding the gun firmly to his side, every bit the gunslinger. If he could see himself from a distance—head down, gun heavy in his hand, still wearing most of a $3,000 suit—he might be ashamed. But he can't, so he isn't. It is just that simple.

†

It is a merlot, purchased for under ten dollars in a grocery store. Maybe it is thin, maybe there is an acid residue in the very front portion of the tongue. Mariah does not pay attention to such things and is, more often than not, the better for it. She swirls the wine in a large tumbler meant for stronger spirits and flips through the channels. She stops on the dating show where a woman with pre-posterous breasts—brazenly round and implanted—has to choose between three men named Rob, or else some reasonable facsimile of it. Bobby. Roberge. Etc. One has blond hair. She won't choose him. Sergio, Mariah's fourteen-year-old Calico, creaks over to her spot on the loveseat. He hops up in slow motion and settles with his face in hers. "Are you getting fresh, Casanova?" she asks in the high-pitched squeak she reserves especially for the cat. He licks his paw, begins to knead himself into her lap. "Christ!" she snorts. "I can not fucking do this on a Friday night." She displaces the cat and grabs the phone, willing Roger to answer.

†

He has positioned himself just right. The timing has to be impeccable. Knock with the left hand, which will then linger to block the
peephole. The right hand holds the gun, barrel pressed a quarter inch
into his temple. Then come the sounds of unlatching. The give of the
door, a crack of light into the dim hallway. Roger's smell floods out—
his hand-rolled tobacco cigarettes, his garlic and herbs—a strong
conglomeration of scents that might seem incongruous attached to
such a slight man. When you knew him, all that changed. You knew
him and his strength was the only thing you knew him by. That is
why Phillip will pull the trigger immediately—there will be a click
or there will be a bang. Either way, it will be something. Either way,
Roger has no choice but to watch what Phillip is willing to do of his
own accord. Phillip finally knocks. He knocks again, poised. After
a short while, there are footsteps behind the door. Then the latches
unlatching, the crack, the slow swing of the door and a wash of
yellow light.

†

Ryan scribbles and, at a particularly furious moment, he throws his head back and bellows. Roars, like a cartoon lion.

†

Eyes already closed, Adele crawls down from her chair, television shining into the room as a single blue moan. She puts her ear to the hard, wooden floor and hears nothing at all. She sinks into a perfectly dreamless, black sleep.

†

When Phillip pulls the trigger—nothing but another click—Roger starts, blinking his eyes and hopping back just slightly. The bullet still hides in the chamber, but the hammer of such a large gun can make an unyielding sound all the same.

"That was the stupidest trick yet, Phil." Roger stares, wide-eyed, straight into Phillip's face. Phillip is sweaty. To Phillip, Roger's head has never seemed more round than it does at this moment, never more perfect, and Phillip feels a surge of something on the order of hate.

"Jesus, I never thought I'd have the chance to say this with a straight face," Roger says. "Give me the gun."

Phillip pulls the trigger again, this time more carelessly, pushing the gun toward his head. Another click. Again Roger flinches. He makes a move toward Phillip then stops. He slumps his shoulders, exasperated, almost laughing.

"You really do think I'm the one who gets hurt by this."

Phillip says the only thing he can think of: "You're a cocksucker."

"Yes."

"Fuck you, Roger."

"You're a walking, talking soap opera. Phillip, stop this."

"You have a tiny penis."

"I'm closing the door."

"Bullshit, you are." Phillip points the gun at Roger.

Roger smiles. "Oh," he says. He pushes the door open and stands before Phillip. His threadbare t-shirt and paper-thin soccer shorts accentuate his thin, hairy limbs.

"Okay, Phillip," he says, now smiling. "I'm ready."

Phillip stands there, waiting.

"You didn't expect me to say that, did you?"

Phillip looks at Roger's perfect head.

"Did you hear me, Phil?" asks Roger. "I'm ready for you to shoot me."

Phillip chews his lip.

"You're the one," says Roger, and he means to follow it with something on the order of "who's not ready," but Phillip doesn't give him the chance. Pained with doubt, Phillip decides that he had better do something. He squeezes the trigger and he can nearly feel the bullet slide into place, ready to fire down the barrel. He doesn't aim, just squeezes, and in an instant that one bullet—the only bullet he's brought, the one he halfheartedly meant to bury in his own gray matter—disintegrates Roger's clavicle. The thin man stumbles to his knees. All either of them can say, until the phone rings moments later, is *Christ, Christ almighty, Christ.*

†

The phone rings and rings, the full six rings. At the sixth, the machine picks up and the short recording—*I'm not here; leave a message if you must*—is drowned out by this symphony of noises:

—Roger, still crouched by the door, looking for all the world as if he's lost a contact lens, saying, alternately, one or two permutations of *Christ* and *I'm having trouble breathing.*

—The click of a still preoccupied Ryan—*What rhymes with cherubim?*—unlatching his door to investigate the loud bangs of the outside world.

—Phillip's short sobs followed by panicked interjections such as, *Sweetie, stop saying that, I know, you're shot through the goddamn chest, of course you can't breathe,* and *Who the fuck picks now to call?*

—Mariah thumping down the steps in her pajama pants with *Jesus that sounded like a gun or something,* then her hand to her mouth and running in place while the shrieks and tears make their way up from somewhere in her center.

The answering machine records it all. Mariah has brought her cordless phone with her down the stairs. She holds it against her chest as if it is her half-escaped heart. Later, if they care to, they can remember the unfortunate events exactly as they sounded to the outside world. When Roger returns from the hospital, he can have them all over to a potluck—perhaps even Adele might come—and they can get tipsy and maudlin and listen to it over and over and over. What they will all forget is that in the midst of their unrest, thunder began to rumble softly outside, followed shortly by a full-fledged warm rain, which drowned out, for a while at least, the burning smells and sounds of an otherwise occupied city.

Venus

The One was the one who could drive the van and no other.
   "Can one of us drive?" we asked once.
   "No yous. Fuck *yous!*—you mouth-breathers…"
And so we didn't drive the van. Never.

The plump one, towards the end, was the one who gave me chills.
My cousin Adele had a lazy eye and she lisped. It made me sad these
things, when I was a child. Because the world was just a mean place.
Even then, I knew that. And the plump one might as well have been
Adele. Her skin tasted of salt.

Many young men cannot say what I can say: I have visited all forty-
eight contiguous states. Canada and Mexico, too. Plus I've stared
across both oceans. The One was adamant about our development as
human men and I must give him credit. He made us read Ayn Rand
and *Don Quixote* and Melville's great whaling text, for these reflected
his philosophy of things and because he believed the heavy stream
of words, page after page, would steel up our minds. And it did.
   I have seen the insides of a human body. I have lived inside someone else's dream.

There was a boy in second grade who lit his own right hand on fire. Sometimes in our travels I believed that this boy was me. *You told that story before and that aint even you.* That's what I would tell myself later. I didn't know what to believe anymore. What I knew is that from nearly the beginning, my right hand ached from the cold, that it would never be the same again.

That, boys, respectively is the face of Lincoln and Roosevelt and Washington and Jefferson and these, yes, are the bad, bad lands. See their blank stares. Burn it in your mind. That's where your rage comes from. They stand by stone-faced and unfinished and do nothing. Them, the ones that let loose this awful corner of the world!

He talked in this manner. He coached us up. We were his ragtag army. He admired our dirty faces. We were made empty so he could fill us up.

Time in the van was the same sort of time as in a dream or a deep space probe. It separated you. *Never* is so much bigger than anything else can ever be. There would *never* not be the van. We would *never* not be driving. The One was methodical about it. Harrowing the sick world is not a vocation to be rushed. It is singular and slow, interpersonal and awful by nature and necessity.

That they believed us to be sexual deviants irked him. That they believed us to be devils, witches, irked him. That the composite sketches were indeterminate, all of us an Everyman, anyone—in this he found the validation he needed.

I remember them in pieces. One liked measured sips of grape soda and smiled too much. One's eyes went dead long before her body did. Several were the other way, with living eyes that had no business still being alive. One's broad back was a field of tiny black moles. All the fingers, the neckties, the ball caps, the brassieres. Commonly we fielded curses, when the point of no return was clear. The world is an awful place. On this we did agree. But—or because of this—I began to make an extended inquiry as to beauty. *Handsome is as handsome does* is what He told us, me. That seemed like too few words. Or words, it seemed, would not do at all.

And that is when I began to fashion my idol out of stone. She fit inside my pocket. She had no feet or hands. I made the rest of her forms exaggerated so that I could hold her in my cold right hand and differentiate her parts. This lobe of breast then that one, her deep navel and full round belly, the mound that dives down into where her thighs meet, then knee-pudge. For an immeasurable period—a haze of white dust clouding up my mind—she was just the pale limestone I was carving her from in this stolen but still timeless time. A wide gap between what I believed and what she really was. Half-formed, she became something, an evolution. She became all of them then the mother of them and then, dug fully from the stone and polished smooth, for some time she became just the one of them: the plump one who was and was not my cousin Adele. Finally she was just the heft of her, what I could feel with my eyes closed in the dark. Wheel noise, the highway underneath us. The soundless weight of the world. I painted her red because red is a live color. She accompanied me undiscovered for many miles.

You mouth-breathing ingrate fuck. Who told you you could fashion such a thing? Who told you you could gather a graven image unto yourself? Don't you ask no questions. Don't you think a goddamn thing again.

I saw her, arcing, somersaulting. She bounced, bold and high up from the black asphalt. And then she shattered into a hundred pieces against the grill of an advancing four-door sedan. She disintegrated into the median, the shoulder even, high into the heavy green trees. The rest of it, I had to imagine. We were always speeding away from what we had broken apart. They tied my hands behind my back, knocked my head to blackness. I was as good as dead.

†

The afterlife: Mile Marker 239.

        And I was set out. Roughly. Forever. A good distance past the only thing I had ever thought to make for myself. And no matter because it had been disintegrated. Into bits. The van fishtailed, spat the gravelly shoulder at me. One stone broke my lip. The thing that was wrong with me drove away. I didn't know anything or where I could go. It was different now. I would never be the same. The world was open to me and I could go anywhere, and it was dark, pitch black, and it was very cold.

Joy

The fat man takes the chopsticks up in both his hands. He stirs the wasabi into his puddle of soy sauce.

"Had you ever seen anyone eat an avocado like that?"

The younger, thinner man takes his pair of sticks in his deft right hand and plucks up a piece of Spider Roll. "Never. It was something. Do you think he'll meet us?"

"It depends on Joy, doesn't it?"

"I've never met her," says the younger man.

"I keep forgetting," says the fat man. He mauls the Supercrunch. "She's just lovely. I could eat her up with a spoon."

"Do tell."

"She's wispy," says the fat man. "And brilliant. I don't know what she's doing with him."

"He's brilliant too."

"Historians aren't brilliant," says the fat man. He is chewing now. "They're dull."

"He didn't eat that avocado dully. I've never seen anyone eat an avocado like that."

"Well, it's not any nevermind to me. I hope he comes. I hope he brings her because she's a delight."

The two men chew large hunks of rice and fish while their suppers cook. They are the only patrons in the restaurant. It has rained. A humid summertime rain. The evening sky is gunmetal blue. The fat man sits at an angle that allows him a view of the large, dormant football stadium. Everything has a bombed-out, empty feeling. The one waitress in the restaurant comes to fill their water glasses.

"I think I'll have another glass of wine. Another for you?"

"Please."

And they eat their fish and drink their wine and wait for the other man to show himself. Halfway through their curried duck, they decide he is not coming. This gives the fat man carte blanche.

"I guess I can say it now," he says. "I think there's trouble in that relationship."

"Which relationship?"

"His and hers," he says.

"How can you know? They just moved here. He hasn't even started the semester."

"Tonight's not the first night I've had him to the porch for drinks," says the fat man. "They've both been over several times. Cooked them dinner once."

"Well aren't you the one-man neighborhood welcoming committee."

"You don't live alone in a house like mine and not entertain."

"And we're all lucky you take such a magnanimous stance on the matter."

The fat man ignores the thin man's cheeky tone. He lunges for a forkful of duck, chews with purpose for a while, and then spits this out: "I know people. I'm an excellent judge of character, and I can tell you that those two are not happy."

"I can't think of anyone who is," says the young man. "Anybody who'll pick up and move here is running from something."

"From Old Virginia, no less," says the fat man.

"Oh good god, why on earth would they leave there for here?" The young man swirls the last of his second glass of wine and downs it.

"I think it's a man."

"Her?"

"Him."

"You just want everybody to be gay."

"I know people."

†

They do not have the Thai ice cream for dessert. Instead, they settle up the bill and wander across the street to the windowless, gray bar pocked with staples from long-gone flyers advertising cover bands. Inside, it is infested with graduate students—humanities types, who should be reading something or another, or grading bad undergraduate papers. The fat man bellies up to the bar and orders a gin and tonic; the young, thin man gets a bottle of pissy light beer. They both sip and eye the darts competition. After a long silence between them, the fat man starts in again.

"Once, she told me a secret," he says. "About him."

"You're ruining him for me," says the young man. "How can I give him a fair shake when I hear all this gossip before I even get to know him?"

"It's not gossip. It's the truth."

"Gossip has nothing to do with whether it's true or not. It's a sentiment."

"Do you want to hear it or not?"

"You're going to tell me either way, so just out with it."

"He cries. All the time. Brushing his teeth. Driving to the pharmacy. After sex. There's not a situation he won't cry in."

The young man pauses with the bottle at his lips. He seems unsure of what to say. The fat man continues.

"I told her a lot of women would kill to have a man who could cry. Do you want to know what she said? I found it very interesting."

"Tell me."

"She said that no woman looks at a man with half as much respect after she's seen him cry."

"She *said* that?" asks the young man. "Good Christ, she's a ball-buster."

"I know. You wouldn't have thought to hear something like that from her. Wispy. Those intelligent spectacles. It's simply not her politics. And do you want to know the worst thing?"

"There's something worse?"

"Oh yes, much worse," says the fat man. "He *heard* her."

The young man blanches, horrified.

"I know," says the fat man, "I know. It was all I could do to pull the situation together. He'd been in the bathroom and was just standing at the screen door. Who knows how long he'd been there, but I knew from the way his shoulders drooped that he'd heard enough."

"What on earth did you do?"

"Refilled drinks. And made a bunch of noise doing it. I think I talked about juniper berries. I felt sure he was going to cry right then. Thank God in Heaven he didn't. I don't think I could have had them back if he did."

"God," says the young man. "What did she do?"

"Smiled a kind of smirk and when he came to sit down next to her, she patted him on the leg as if it never happened. Or maybe precisely because it did."

The two men look at each other. One starts giggling, and the other can't help himself.

†

Outside, the men begin their walk home. The evening is hot from the moisture in the air, and the fat man must unbutton the top three buttons on his damp oxford shirt. He limps just slightly and he is full of food and drink. The young man has to be careful not to outpace his companion. They slowly pass two more bars, a coffee shop. Once they amble past the filling station, they make it to the fringes of the fat man's neighborhood. The houses are old and stately. Inside, warm lights wash over good wood, antique Tabrizes and Najafabads.

"These places aren't just houses," says the tiring fat man. "They're homes."

"You sound like a Realtor."

"I would've been a good one," the fat man says. "I know people."

There is something slightly different to the ordinary evening smell of burning rubber from the tire factory across the river. It is more smoky, more pleasant. The fat man attributes this aloud to the moisture in the air. The thin man disagrees silently. It is something else that he can't yet place. They walk on, past more houses that are homes, down this street and that one. Soon they hear the huge screech of sirens. The smoke smell is more pronounced.

"Hurry," says the fat man, "something's on fire in the neighborhood."

"Easier said than done," says the younger man.

The fat man ignores him and picks up the pace as best he can. Really there is no increase in pace—just a few more wiggles and gyrations as he pumps his arms in a faux hustle. There are more sirens and before long, they see the smoke. Large, billowing gray mounds of it.

"Oh, God, not my house," yelps the fat man. "Goddamn it I live for that house!"

"I'll run ahead," says the younger man.

"What good does that do me?" asks the fat man.

"I'll find out which house it is and I'll run back."

"Fine, do whatever you want. I'm going as fast as I can."

"If you had a phone…"

"For Christ's sake, don't be ridiculous. We're talking about a matter of seconds. A minute at most. A cellular telephone at a time like this. Who on earth could I call?"

He lets the thought trail off because he can see, up ahead, a police car has blocked off the road.

"Good Lord, there's no way through. We'll have to find another way."

They circle back around and hit the main thoroughfare, shuffle down the long strip that leads into and out of town, and finally make it to the fat man's street, several blocks away from his house. More sirens blare and, at the tree line down the road, the sky is a hazy orange.

"My poor cat," says the fat man.

"Calm down," the younger man says. "There are dozens of houses on this street."

"I just know it. I can feel it. Like a part of me is gone."

They push ahead and, for all the younger man's reassurances, the fire does seem to be coming from the general vicinity of the fat man's beloved house. The young man pictures all the careful clutter—the stacks of good, thick books, the knick-knacks and trinkets. Such just-so accumulation can never be replaced. They make their way closer to the commotion that is brewing around several houses on either side of the fire. The young man feels a drier, warmer rush of air on his face. Up this close, they both see quite clearly that it is not, in fact, the fat man's house that is on fire. For one thing, the fire is coming from the left-hand side of the street—almost directly across from the fat man's house. The fat man lets out a little sound from deep in his throat—a faint but exultant sigh. Then the two of them begin to calculate: if it isn't the fat man's house, whose is it?

"I see Joy," says the fat man. He picks up the pace—this time legitimately—points vaguely. The young man hangs back, letting his companion lead the way. He sees a woman, tall, slender, and a dog pacing nervously at her feet. She is crouched over at the waist, her hands cupped together at her heart. Her body convulses in a familiar rhythm. Soon they are close enough to hear her. She is not just sobbing. She is giving herself over to something. The fire, perhaps. She is letting herself become unraveled in the face of the warm, orange light. A firefighter stands near her, halfway comforting her. Neighbors are everywhere, taking in the grand and awesome display. A burning house, a woman outside watching her home burn. She could not be more beautiful. The dog whines nervously. The fat man stops next to another man who holds a pad.

"Where is he?"

"He's in there," says the man. "Cops say he put the dog in the car with a note. Booby-trapped the place so no one can go in after him."

"Good god," says the fat man. His chest is heaving from the exertion. "Sweet Jesus."

Absently, the fat man walks to his own house. His young companion follows him up the steps and onto the porch. They both sit on the swing, but the fat man pops up.

"I need a drink."

He pulls a bottle from the small refrigerator in the corner of the porch and, hands shaking, pours gin into a plastic cup. He doesn't bother asking his companion if he'd like to join him. Instead he opens the front door to the house and clucks for the cat to come and sit with him. The house across the street still burns and the firefighters mainly let it go—it's too far gone—dousing a ring around it to keep it from spreading to the other houses. The two men watch as the wailing woman is taken away in an ambulance.

"I can't fathom this," says the fat man. "This is too much."

"He was in your kitchen not three hours ago."

"Don't remind me," he says. "It's just too much. I'm sorry. I have to go in."

"Of course."

"You can sit there all night if you want. I just need to go in."

"Yes, I understand. I'll be going in a minute."

"Do what you want," says the fat man, and he scoops up the cat and his gin, and he shuffles to the door.

"Excuse me." It is the man with the pad, standing at the screen. "I couldn't help but overhear. The sound carries off your porch. Did you say you had the man in your house earlier? I'm with the *News*."

"He was wonderful, a brilliant mind," says the fat man. "Quote me on that. 'He was wonderful, a brilliant mind.'"

"Any idea why he would do something like this? Did he say anything this evening?"

"He was in excellent spirits," says the fat man. "Such a gentle man. He had the world to live for. A treasure for a wife. I know people, and I know what a treasure that girl is. My heart goes out to her. You can quote that too." He gives the man his name, excuses himself, and is gone with a snap of the porch light.

But everything is lit up now. The reporter turns around on the stoop but doesn't leave. He watches the fire, as does the young man who sits on the porch swing, the heat of the fire warming their faces. A young woman—a neighbor in the duplex several doors away—has been charged with the dog. The young man watches her use her boyfriend's belt to form a makeshift leash. The dog is skittish and small. It ducks and feints and whines. Finally she abandons the plan and takes the animal up in her arms.

"You wonder what the dog knows," says the reporter.

This is what the young man sees and hears before he heads off into what will become the first in a series of restless nights: a young woman with a stricken look, surprised to have a dog in her arms but intent on doing something to help, not sure whether to laugh or cry when the dog licks her chin. He sees the girl and her beau and the dog walk quickly down the street. The reporter, slowly at first and then quicker, follows. The thin young man doesn't turn to watch him go. He doesn't have to. He just stares into the burning house and the flashing, silent fire truck lights. Soon there is a small but persistent knock-knock-knock in the direction of the duplex. It reverberates once and then again and still another time and then it dies away.

Ruin

It is the coast and it is flat and it, like others, is an American city. Mobile this morning is quiet, warm and green but dead, as if no one at all is noticing its history or grandeur as it sits alone very near a giant, shallow body of water. Sixteen years ago, I was married here. If I had known it was this—slow, an outpost—I would have balked at the symbolism, but I had never been here before. My ex-wife was a small woman, pretty but plain, almost bookish, and she had her nose in a textbook on torts as we sat in the judge's waiting room. (I am now—but was not then—aware of the irony.)

"Are you going to take off your glasses when we exchange vows?"

She looked at me above them, took them off, and leaned over to kiss me on the forehead. Then back to torts, squinting.

†

Silence scares me. Out of an extended silence, the smallest noise becomes magnified. Mobile is quiet this morning. My marriage was quiet. The last eighteen months have been noisy by design. I now spend much of my day in the pressroom, shouting at the stripper, him shouting at me, watching the press, struggling to be heard above the din. The hum stays in my ears long after I get home. I am with a woman named Nicole who is eleven years younger than I am, a waitress who talks by default and who elicits still more talk, either because she is slim and moves like a dancer or because she is easy to flash a flawless smile. More likely both.

Nicole is a Mobile native. I have, until now, resisted accompanying her when she returns for visits, which she does often. (Her mother is ill; her father is retired after thirty-four years working on the docks.) One night early this week, Nicole was eating ice cream from the container. Sitting on the corner of the loveseat she observed, matter of fact, that we have been seeing each other for almost four months now, sleep in the same bed most nights, and don't even go out much except on Saturday nights to the Mexican place for cheap, salty margaritas. So why, she asked—implored—if we're already so damned *domestic*, why make a big deal about going home with her this weekend? Her people, she said, were starting to think she made me up.

I listened to everything, not just to her but to the TV: Robert Novak and Jerry Falwell and then Bill Press on *Crossfire*. First Nicole, then Novak or Falwell or Press. Nicole, them. Them, Nicole. All of these people floated their words into the room and it was a delightful cacophony and I bathed in it. When I was finally ready to address the expectant face of my new lover, I told her that I couldn't possibly go to Mobile because it is too quiet, that I am not a man equipped to handle heavy silences. At this she laughed and pointed her spoon in my direction. She told me I don't know quiet until I've sat where she's sat on any old Tuesday night eating dinner with the likes of me. Then she walked over—slinked over, Nicole slinks, whether she means to or not—and she tousled my hair because she thought, wrongly, that she'd hurt my feelings. Then we made love, listening to Robert Novak rail against "Slick Willy."

Later in the week, because I do not quite have the energy to fight it, I take the time off and we drive to Mobile. The drive down is air and light. Blonde, blue-eyed, garrulous Nicole illuminated by a *National Geographic* sun. There is more beauty in my car than I have a right to. Nicole, the music, the sweet fresh air. There are also her words, which reassure me even when I do not listen to what they say, and her bare foot up on the dash. She tells me everything—things she's said before, new things, tangential things, things she tells me to forget. I say nothing. I tap my fingers on the steering wheel, sometimes put my hand on her knee.

At times like this especially, I have to check off the reasons we are together, for reassurance: there is music—our one true common bond, unabashed album rock from the sixties and seventies, mostly. There is the fact that I am older and gainfully employed—"I don't know if you've noticed," she reassured me after that first night, "but women like older guys. And vice versa. The math isn't hard." Except when I do the math, I see her long, golden legs and her ease with a smile and it doesn't add up. But I am good at not asking questions, so I don't. I keep my hand on her knee.

When we arrive, there is a strange first meal with her parents. Her mother is the kind of conversationalist who turns everything around to herself. Nicole, I can tell, tries not to be embarrassed at this, but it is innocent. There is a certain charm to it. And besides, the woman is slowly, sometimes painfully dying, and so I am happy to give her any small thing that will ease her pains. Her father, on the other hand, turns everything around to me. I had not envisioned him as a mountainous man—6'5", 240 with dinner-plate hands—nor as a soft-spoken interrogator. *Oh, Nicole, your uncle Bill and aunt Judy are planning on visiting for Labor Day—say, Jim, Nicole says you been married once before.* The implied questions: Where is she? What did you do? It was your fault, wasn't it, Jim? You drove her away, what with your stoicism, your stinginess with words? She didn't desire you, did she, Jim? Your body was a neutral thing to her, am I right? By the way, why are you forty-one years old? I know that you have had my daughter, Jim. Don't think I don't know it. Don't think I don't know this is the worst mistake my long-legged, beautiful daughter—who is younger than you and nicer than you and better than you—has ever made.

He smiles at me and kisses Nicole's temple when we leave for the hotel.

"Y'all can always stay here," he says.

"Daddy, that's sweet," Nicole says back. "But we're going to be meeting up with some friends and it'll be late."

We are not meeting friends; we go to our room in the Admiral Raphael Semmes hotel downtown and make love, with an especial vigor, until very late. Still, it was the polite thing for her to say and I'm glad she thought of it. Left to my own devices, I simply would've stared at the man. Or run away.

†

At 7:23 a.m. it is 82°. At this rate, I think to myself, the heat of the day will be painful. Nicole sleeps behind me with just the sheet covering her legs. She is a stomach sleeper. I watch the smooth lines of her rib cage, her back, which rises with a breath, then falls. I have opened the window but the air doesn't move much. At the honking of a bus horn below, Nicole wakes up.

"You're early," she says.

"Couldn't really sleep."

"It's supposed to be me who tires you out." She stretches to her full length with a yawn. Her hair is mussed like a girl's. She walks over to me with the sheet wrapped around her, leans in and kisses me on the mouth. There is a hint of sleep on her breath, and even that tastes good. She walks to the bathroom, eyes almost closed, and drops the sheet just as she crosses the threshold. In the instant before she closes the door behind her, I see her silhouette—long and thin and ageless—and I forget who I am, who she is, or why exactly we are here.

†

"Now I assume both mommas and daddies know what you're doing?"

The judge who married Elizabeth and me was a fat man who had studied law in Tuscaloosa, just as Elizabeth was doing then. He asked about a professor who looked like Tweety Bird. Yes, he was still there. Yes, everyone still called him Tweety Bird. The judge asked again about our parents and accepted our answers, as if such an acceptance was necessary.

"Y'all are young and in love, I can tell that much."

Good, I thought. *But how he can tell for sure?* I hoped it was something in the way Elizabeth looked at me when I wasn't paying attention. Something I hadn't yet seen.

"What's that book you got there, young lady?"

"Torts, your honor."

Torts, your honor. My god.

"You got the bedside manner down, I see. She's a sharp one, young man."

And he laughed and we laughed, but I had no idea what he was talking about. I tried to exchange a look with Elizabeth, but she was transfixed, eyes straight ahead and myopic without her glasses. I'm sure we eventually turned to one another, took each other's hands, and looked each other in the eyes. But she couldn't see me, not really, and I knew it, and she knew I knew it. Later we would both admit that this was the turning point in our marriage. The very instant it set forth blindly into the world.

†

"What do you want to do, baby?"

I try not to melt at the term of endearment. "We have to do something?" I still haven't showered, am still sitting next to the window watching the bank clock give me the bare essentials of the day. 8:01 a.m., now 83°.

Nicole raises her eyebrow. "Of course we do, silly man. Daddy's taking Momma to Dr. Fuller's. They're gonna be gone all day and we're gonna meet them up for dinner at Roussos tonight. We got the whole day to fill."

"I can think of something," I say.

"Oh, no sir. I got my hand on that throttle," Nicole says. "You don't just get sweetness any old time. There's a quid pro quo to this."

She picks up the *Mobile Register* we bought yesterday and starts rifling through it, not really reading it. She looks like a movie star, so I just watch her for a little while.

"What?" she asks me, but her smile is broad because she knows I think she's beautiful.

"Nothing," I say, and look back at the clock.

"Well get in there and wash off the sleep-stink, lazy."

Nicole is this way. She is always, always moving, expecting the same of me, even though that is not my way at all. In the shower, I spin the soap in my hands, lather it up real nice, and smooth it over my face—top to bottom, outside in. Forehead, cheekbones, slide along the jaw. I save the nose for last, go slow, feel my hands slip over its contours.

I start to think about a woman named Anna, whom I have not thought about in a long while. Anna had been a beauty queen in high school and whose face—eyes, smile, teeth—still evidenced it. Other parts of her went this way or that—some parts of her still bore a resemblance to those of a schoolgirl beauty and others did not. She was alluring, at any rate, and I slept with her during the last two years of my marriage.

When it ended, it was a very emotional thing, much more emotional than I had imagined it would be. She wanted to leave her husband, wanted us to go someplace. Arizona. Oregon. Start over. I didn't want that. I just wanted things to stay the same. I asked her what her kids would think. But she was wild-eyed, said everything would work out the way it was supposed to. I said I agreed about that, that everything would work out the way it was supposed to. And it did. I told her I could not, would not, leave with her. Her husband ended up leaving *her* for somebody else in a fit of romance. She took up with the divorce lawyer, getting a huge piece of her husband's landscaping business, and moving to Port St. Lucie, Florida. Of course, she didn't know it was all going to work out when I wouldn't run off with her, so when I told her I could never leave with her, she punched me square in the nose. Broke it right at the center. This was what startled Elizabeth into ending our marriage. There was now permanent evidence of the truth: I was a son of a bitch. I am sure she suspected as much for some time. Now here it was, staring her in the face. Not just my black eyes, the bandages. They went away. The slight angle of the cartilage, its skew and the tiny bump at the breaking point—all of that would be there forever. I have learned that it's mostly the details people can't abide.

†

"Don't you clean up nice," Nicole says, handing me some shorts and a polo. "Wouldn't guess for a minute that you're pushing sixty." She laughs at her joke. That's the kind of thing she says that should cut to the quick, but somehow it doesn't. Somehow it makes you love her, or something like it, and you know she doesn't mean it in an ugly way. "Hurry up and put these on," she says. "I know exactly what we're up to."

I put them on, and comb my hair straight back. It's getting long, and the odd strand of gray is more prominent that way. It makes me rakish, though, even handsome, if I may say so. Nicole smiles at me, like she's read my mind and agrees, and she kisses my cheek.

"Okay?" she asks and grabs my hand, whisks me toward the day.

We get out on the road, and she points to where I need to go until we're on a state highway heading south. I don't bother to ask where we're going because I don't care. The music and the woman beside me are enough. We drive, not saying much, and the green engulfs everything. There is gray asphalt with double yellow lines running through it, but everything else is south Alabama summertime green. And it is hot.

"I could live out here," she says.

"I think you could live just about anywhere," I say.

"I think you're right," she says.

"I know I am."

We pull off the main highway, veer to the left at a sign that points to Bayou La Battre. Locals call it something that sounds almost like Bayou La Battery. Not much to it, except shrimp boats, and that's been a difficult way to go about living for some time. Once a year, though, it's a festival. The Blessing of the Fleet. The archbishop himself attends, waves religious *accoutrement* at the ratty vessels, exhorting God to keep things safe and bountiful. Of course, there's no guarantee of either safety or bounty, but it's a good excuse to get drunk and parade the boats down the channel. That, explains Nicole, is what we're about to do.

"Now you watch if I don't get us on one of them shrimping boats, my dear," she tells me. "Honey, you'd shit a brick."

I've never been on a boat and she knows I don't intend to break that string, so I just shake my head. But I know there will be gumbo there, and other things I like, so I am generally happy and so is Nicole. My hand finds its way onto her bare knee, and her hand finds its way onto mine.

In town—if you can call it that—traffic piles up as everyone waits to pull in around the Baptist church and park in the big field adjacent to the channel. There are all kinds, but mainly working people. The men have tattoos and the women wear their hair long in the back and short on the top and sides. So do the men. There are Harleys, there are pick-ups. This is not to say there aren't families here—there are—and there are some who are taking in the local color, as we are. But this is mostly of, by, and for Bayou La Battrians. There is a bluegrass band playing, and they are playing well, and the smell of cooked fish and shrimp and good spices makes me feel safe.

"It's a party, baby," she says as we park and get out. I squeeze her hand a little bit, but only so she will stop talking. Everyone, everyone in the place, is noticing. I can imagine it spreading through the throngs like wildfire: There is an old man here, and he has on his arm a divine presence, long and lithe. Come. Come see it. They are not from here.

These, though, are imaginings, and so I try not to indulge them. I feel Nicole's hand in mine and let that tether me. I look for things that aren't people. In the channel, the boats that will take part in the parade are filled with people. There is nowhere to look that is not people. One little boat, set off some from the rest, houses a happy delegation of Vietnamese. They are the ones with the green bottles of Heineken when everybody else has cans of pissy domestic beer. They make a sound unlike the rest. Happy, like the rest, but the tenor of it is not the same. More cacophonous. Theirs is the only boat that doesn't have music piping out loud. They are happy enough with the noises they make.

We find the entrance to the church where they're selling gumbo and shrimp by the pound for cheap. There is the respite of a long line. Nicole and I do not say much. She just smiles, as if this is exactly where she is supposed to be, and I just smell the smells. When we get to the food, I order gumbo and slices of bread, and she gets a pound of shrimp. The idea is that we'll share, but when we get outside and sit by a big oak tree, I eat the gumbo and she eats the shrimp. The gumbo is thin. The shrimp looks bland.

"You want some beer?" I ask, and point to the beer stand.

"You are the picture of a gentleman," she says, a faux belle.

So we get beer. I have to pee, so I hand her my beer and she says she'll find us a place closer to the canal. I say, "In the shade, if you can," and she waves as she walks away from me, not bothering to turn around. I take a minute to enjoy her walking away from me.

Finding her when I get out isn't a problem—she's under the most conspicuous tree around, sitting on a blanket, laughing with what looks to be a sixteen-year-old, shirtless boy. He is thin and tall for his age and his body is hairless and his shining blond hair is longer, even, than mine. He is, goddamn it, beautiful and audacious.

"Hey, baby," she says to me, handing me the beer. "Jesse here was nice enough to let us borrow an extra blanket. Wasn't that sweet?"

"It was," I say, and that's all. I wait for him to say something stupid, to ask me if I am Nicole's uncle or father, something that will necessitate a scene. But he doesn't.

"Glad y'all came down," he says instead. He shakes my hand without getting up. "We like it when we get to entertain good folks who ain't from here. More of a show that way."

It doesn't take me long to figure out that Jesse means nothing by any of this. If he could, he would ravish Nicole. Surely he knows I know that. But he doesn't know how to ravish her, only that he *wants* to, and there is a wide gulf between the two.

"Y'all should come over and sit with me and my friends," he says instead. "We got plenty of beer, and we already staked out the best place to watch the boats go by. They're about to start up."

Nicole wants to, I can tell from the way her mouth opens in surprise. She is not a bad person because she wants to. That's not it at all. The things I am thinking—her and Jesse under this very tree, in the hot day, alone, their perfect skin, perfect noses, perfect mouths, joined in a slick, more perfect union—do not even enter her mind. She is not, after all, a man. She is a woman who likes company, who likes to be happy and to be with happy people. But I don't want to be with Jesse anymore, so I say so.

"That's real nice of you, Jesse," I say. "You're a good fellow for asking, but we plan to get on a boat."

With this, Nicole is giddy like a little girl and my spirit is flying because I have made her that way. I feel desperate, too, because I am certain I will fail to get us on a boat, but I take her by the hand and head for the canal anyway. She whoops a happy little goodbye to Jesse, running just behind me with her long, conspicuously graceful strides. We have to dodge around people spread out on blankets and in lawn chairs. The commotion upsets them, I think, but we head on a beeline for the channel. I have an idea of where to go.

When we get there, we stop short and Nicole bumps into me. She laughs a little then stares at the boat. The Vietnamese are silent, all of them staring at us. Nicole looks at them like they are extraterrestrial and, perhaps, at this time and place, they are the next closest thing. While we consider one another, the captain of the ship slowly breaks into a bright, golden-toothed smile. He says something, at which I nod and point to Nicole and myself, then to the boat. He shrugs and waves us on board. Nicole lets out delighted thank-you's in all directions and wraps herself around the captain's neck. He stumbles back, makes a big show of it, laughs, hugs her. Everybody laughs. The cacophony rings out again, their particular kind of music. I am handed a cold green bottle. The children tug at Nicole's shorts, stand on the side of the boat and play with her blonde hair. It's not long before all the boats begin to pull out. We back away from the dock, awkward at first, causing a great commotion in the one large boat behind us. Then the captain rights us, steadies us. Everything else recedes: Jesse, the archbishop, the boat behind us, all our assorted failures. The Vietnamese, Nicole—everyone falls silent. Soon we hear nothing—we listen for nothing—but the steady growl of the motor pushing us down the channel and toward the bright, wide-open gulf.

Blackface

Cindy Newman comes face to face with her nineteen-year-old son, Charlie, only it is in the house of a man who is not his father. It is late in the night, the house is dark and she, almost inexplicably—except for the ubiquity of whims and predilections—, stands before him nude, wearing a bowler. In the manner of minstrel shows, her face is smeared with black grease paint. Upstairs, Ken Martin, a widower and a neighbor, waits for her. She has gone to retrieve candles and matches from his kitchen, stumbling on high heels through the dark. Charlie is drunk and when he is drunk, he sometimes chances to wander through houses and steal things. He has entered the Martin house through the unlocked back door, been stumbling around himself for five minutes. He has two candleholders stuffed in his pants, and his pockets jangle with the other trinkets he's found so far. Now, as this strange apparition turns into the living room, he sways in the face of her fullness. A dim white streetlight shines through the front window, across her torso. Behind her is a picture of Ken's dead wife, their two married-off sons. Charlie can see Cindy's chin clearly, that it is a shiny, dark thing set against her creamy skin. Her unruly blond curls spill against it. She is anyone but his mother in such a disguise. Cindy knows her son, though, even in the dark: his wiry frame, the set of his shoulders in the face of a puzzle. They stand, transfixed, for several long seconds, each expecting something from the other—a mad crash through a window, a long, high wail.

Then she lets herself think it, just for a moment. *What does he want from me*—? She recalls his body as a small child, how soft and pink. He was so beautiful as a little boy, she had the not-uncommon impulse to consume him. Now she says his name softly in the dark, a kind of question. He answers by swimming across a loveseat and ottoman, the holders spilling loudly from his pants. He bolts past her through the house, out the back door, and into the plain, open night. He is still drunk, still unsure of exactly what he has seen and why.

Delivered

He will later wonder how it all played out this way. Two pepperonis to an apartment in a neighborhood where they don't tip. He jumps down the steps, knocks—here is where he goes wrong: the invitation inside. He puts the pizzas on the table, smiles at the little Mexican—Mexican?—boy, who smiles back. Somehow, waiting to get paid, he comes to be in the center of the room. Then, flooding from the one room in the back, seven, eight men come walking. *Banditos*, he thinks. One thrusts something—a package, a small satchel?—into his arms, laughs and points to the ceiling. A rooster—yes, a rooster—now grips the pizza boy's fingers as he holds the bird over his head. The bird is heavy and has gold feathers on his belly. It doesn't try to fly. Or squawk. Just sits in his palms, black pebbles pressed into its head for eyes. Moving its neck in darts, quick feints like a boxer. And the bird's owner, a small, dark man with a square jaw, stately and tenement-poor, grins widely with very many teeth. The little boy translates: *He wants you to hold the rooster higher—hold him high over your head.* The man moves his eyes up to the bird and smiles a wider smile. The rooster is calm. It purrs. *This bird fights very well—he's never been beaten.* The smiling man clucks his tongue twice, quickly, softly. Like he's scolding a lover. Pascal—this is the rooster's name—looks down at the boy's father, eyes now burning coals, as if he knows the words *fights* and *beaten*. In a red flash of feathers, wings, the bird leaps from the pizza boy's hands. He feels the exact moment the bird is gone—its heft and then its nothing. The bird lands with a great thud against the man's chest. Calm again, almost immediately, like all great killers.

Yoi, Hajime

The year is two thousand and one. I am in Beppu City, Japan, with a tiny yellow chick in my hands. Strangely, my thoughts are in Atlanta, Georgia. America, the nineteen-sixties. An odd place for a Japanese to be. It was wonderful. Glorious. In the evenings, after my work, I would go to the baseball field to watch Henry Aaron and eat a hot-dog. I have not eaten a hotdog in some time, though I love them. A hotdog, to me, means Atlanta. 755 homeruns.

Under the hot light, surrounded by a hundred other sexers, I stare at the chick's underside, apply a hint of pressure. A drop of excrement bubbles out. The cloaca is exposed and the genitalia are there to interpret. Like tea leaves. It is an intuition, almost; more than anything else, a divination. Pullet. Cockerel. Pullet. Pullet. One hundred of them in this way in less than four minutes. Slower has no chance of winning.

There was a time when the sexing of chicks was a marketable skill. $500 a day. People have always wanted a pullet's sweeter, softer meat. But if there is a way to do something faster and cheaper, it will be found. Americans will find it. Now it is by feathers—the females bred for longer wings. A monkey can distinguish them now. Koreans, Mexicans—anybody does the work.

†

The hot summers of Georgia invigorated me—its steam. The people themselves had this heat slow-baked into them. The blacks, especially, were fascinating in this way. I fell in love with their skin, their slow movements and the eyes with such graceful anger. This is, actually, too broad. There is one woman with whom I fell in love, one woman whose skin and slow movements entranced me, whose eyes shot brown sparks through me.

I am an old man—growing old, anyway—and can be forgiven some romance, the exotic and purple prose of a brief and unrequited American love. She was Lucy. She worked in the hatchery, sorting eggs. The length of a dancer and short-cropped hair. I did not speak to her directly, of course. Not at first. I would not have spoken to her first had she been Japanese—not even if a myriad of circumstances hadn't dictated against it. But they did: language, culture, time. In this instance, there was little I could do. If the truth is to be told, I would not have known what to do with an American woman. A woman like Lucy. But part of my duties was to teach others to sex the chicks. I was young and sly and my time in America was limited. I told my superior that Lucy was one of the workers who looked right for the new work.

When she came to me, she was silent and impatient. We exchanged very few words in those first days. I pointed and gestured instead. My English was passable, but she didn't expect me to speak and I was nervous, so I fell back on ignorance. Lucy's fingers were long. She squeezed too hard on the bellies of the chicks.

"Too much," I told her. It was one of her last chicks of that first day.

"I'll say it's too much," she said. "They shit like it's going out of style."

†

The lamp is so close to my forehead, it almost burns the skin. I can feel it turning red in one spot. My wife and daughters are in attendance. I lean my head forward for a long moment until I touch the bulb and jolt back in my chair. One person gasps. Everyone else ignores me. The sexers sex. It is in these moments, when I am doing something by rote, that my mind floats back to things like Atlanta, forms like Lucy's. And I am a sexer. Everything I do is by rote.

There is a fantasy that has, over the years, taken the shape of a recurrent dream. Material and sensual. I am lying in the thick, spongy grass of a Georgia centerfield. It is a cool evening. Baseballs float over my head, one by one, and crash into the empty outfield bleachers. Lucy walks to me, kneels, touches my head and my hair. She smiles. Even in her eyes, she smiles at me.

†

"Who cuts your hair, Ricky?"

She called me Ricky. My Japanese name was too difficult for her to say. Junichi became Ricky. I didn't mind. It was nice to be something only to her.

I told her I didn't know who cut my hair. A man in a shop near where I lived.

"I'll cut your hair next time," she said. "It looks like he puts a bowl on your head."

I asked her if she ever cut hair for a living.

"First of all," she laughed, "I wouldn't be squeezing shit out of chickens if I cut hair for a living. Second, you should be happy to get anybody but that old man with the bowl."

I enjoyed the attention. Of course.

All told, my time with Lucy was quite short. A matter of a few weeks, perhaps less. I remember very few things about her now—only her vague shape and the feeling in my throat when she walked into the room. I remember, too, that she was inept at sexing. A chick seemed to sense it was in the wrong hands as soon as she picked it up. A squirming ball of yellow fuzz, excrement streaming out of a hole almost no one in the world can see.

But in those few weeks, Lucy began to talk more and more. It was a strange thing—the Americans often talked openly to me. I am sure it had something to do with foreignness, a feeling that I could not hurt them. If I could even understand them, the fact that I was Japanese cancelled out any hold I could claim over them. I did, in fact, understand many of them, even if the language was spotty. Lucy especially, probably because I wanted to understand her more than the others.

She started talking to me in earnest by telling me about her mother, who was a seamstress until she had a stroke and could no longer concentrate for long periods of time. Her grandmother was also a seamstress—a successful one, at that, who had even owned her own shop, but eventually it failed for no particular reason. "She hated sewing after that," Lucy told me. "Like it was a punishment."

For that reason, Lucy told me, she didn't sew. She didn't do anything particularly well, by design. "Even if I could do something better than anybody, I wouldn't want to. It let's you down. You'll see, Ricky."

†

The box of chicks is silent. The room is silent. My wife stares at me, a constant half-smile slapped across her face. Then the sound comes back in a rush: chicks peeping madly, constantly, the room a cacophony of sexers and chicks and judges walking the rows. A shuffle or cough from the audience punctuates our odd symphony. This is one of the moments when I remember that particular conversation with Lucy. *You'll see*, she had told me. At the time, I had known she would be right, but I was lost other than that. I did not know what I would see, or when, or why.

For quite some time, I could not remember what had spurred us to talk about such things. Most often, our conversations were Lucy's soliloquies on American television or on the precise way to make a peanut butter and jelly sandwich. I was a fascinated bystander, soaking in her rich, soft voice and singing inside at her laugh which could only be described as a cackle.

But here, Beppu City, in the All-Japan championships, I recall our only significant exchange, word for word. Lucy and I are thirty years older, almost exactly a world away from each other, and now I relive our only real intercourse. The chicks go silent again.

†

Lucy sat in a chair across the room from me as I sexed. It was late in her time with me—in a matter of a few days, she would be gone. First from my tutelage, then from the hatchery altogether. She had, for several days, spent more of her time talking than working with the chicks. This, of course, did not bother me. I did my best to increase my own output, so they wouldn't take her away for not doing the work. (Eventually, they did just that.)

She leaned her head back as far as she could, stretching her legs out to their full, dramatic length. She spread her arms wide like wings and yawned. The smooth brown skin of her neck held me stunned for a moment. She stayed like that for while, watching the ceiling with eyes that, for an instant, looked like a child's. Then she snapped to and brought her limbs in to sit and stare at me.

"You tell me something."

I glanced at her, and went back to examining the chick in my hands—a pullet, it turned out.

"I don't even know how you learned to do this crazy business you do."

I couldn't help but smile as I reached for another chick. It started slowly, my own soliloquy. At first, she asked questions here and there, then she sat and listened, her expression unchanging. I told her that my profession had been an accident—far from some ancient tradition passed down through my family. My father had been an auto mechanic, my mother a teacher. The day before my graduation ceremony from secondary school, I saw an ad for sexing in a magazine. Something as simple as that. My parents were crushed that I would not attend college. But it was a profession, a skill. The sureness involved in that. I wanted, more than anything then, for my life to begin.

That is when she told me, sitting in the same position, her face plain, of her mother and grandmother. Of her own philosophy of work. *You'll see*, she told me.

As I have said, I knew that I would see, if not what. I knew it plainly and it broke my heart. I wanted nothing more than to scoop her up in my arms and run away from the hatchery. We could run through the hot streets, hand in hand. We would laugh for no reason. Running and running, we would wind through the city and then out of it. Before us, like magic, would be Fulton County Stadium and there would be a baseball game with Henry Aaron and hotdogs. I would buy two hotdogs and we would walk up the concourse to our seats. Henry Aaron would hit nothing but homeruns. We would walk to the field in the late innings, lie in the grass.

Even as my mind settled back into the room, the hatchery, I thought to ask her if she would go somewhere with me. Maybe even a baseball game. But I didn't. I knew the answer would be no and I could not bear to have to remember that. So now, instead, I remember almost nothing. A fleeting glimpse of her neck. Snippets of conversation. The taste of hotdogs. An almost tragic juxtaposition.

†

I have gone fast—too fast. I have beaten my own personal best by more than twenty seconds. When I call the judge over to report my time, a gasp goes up. They believe I have beaten the decades-old record of three minutes, six seconds. In this age of a declining profession, such news would be a vindication—at least a brief visitation from our glorious past. I know it is not so. Not only have I missed the time, I have made many errors. I can feel it—can almost count them and, if I had the chance, I could return to my boxes of chicks and point out the ones who had been sexed incorrectly. The verification returns—seven errors. A particularly large number. The crowd groans. My wife—she has been a good woman to me—smiles a simple smile in my direction.

The Scrivener

My drama.—This is a missive, written in snatches. It is better that you do not know exactly who I am or what I do. These things cloud a philosophy such as this. Invariably hints will struggle to the surface—that I am a business traveler, for instance; that on this particular trip I have elected, as is the current trend in American hotels, to "save water and BTUs" by sleeping on the same linens for the duration of my short stay. Do not allow these things to wrestle your attention away.

These are the bare essentials: I was born on the East Coast. My parents never moved, never altered vocation or avocation, and so my sisters and I learned very early that life is an inexorable march. Slow and plain. Toward what, none of us was quite sure. At least I wasn't. As a boy I was nondescript and did nondescript things: Scouts, bicycles. And then after several of life's obstacles—college, an aborted engagement, a job or two of increasing, if generally vague, responsibilities—I came to be here. To sit on this chair in this particular room, nineteen stories above the Great Midwestern City.

Outside, there is a gray faux ocean. There is what I would call a trickle of traffic for a Monday morning rush. Today I have a meeting, a presentation regarding such things as "indemnity." When my colleague calls down—we will refer to him as "Larry," for ease—I am to meet him in the lobby and we will proceed. His call is forty-five minutes away. Forty-five minutes from right now. Slow, inexorable.

8:04 a.m.—This place, from up here, looks especially scrubbed at the end of winter. The tiny municipal golf course, wedged between skyscrapers, abutments, and major thoroughfares, sits brown and undefended and alone. It is something like the doe of lore who sneaks her way into a Manhattan somewhere, just before she is recognized for what she is: a wide-eyed anomaly.

There are also gulls swirling, and the Great Water. A blackish tributary winds through the city, then it bleeds into a gray shore and then further and further out, into the expanse, until it all becomes a faint blue horizon-wide line.

It is the morning and bright, though overcast, and the city is awake. In the tower across from mine, there is only one lamp left on from the previous night. It is far away and I don't see well but, during the night, I could make out two figures at this very window. They barely moved as I watched for nearly twenty minutes, trying to make out the scene. Were those flesh tones? Was that a kind of pose? They did not come together, never touched as far as I could tell. I gave up my watching. Now, though, with the telltale sign of unnecessary light, all possible ends to the story exist.

8:09 a.m.—At the other end of this small room is another view. This of the clean city streets. I spy a bundled man. I spy cold smoke and terraces, a crane. There are small satellite dishes, perched on railings, and there is a trolley and scaffolding and beyond that—beyond all of it—is the behemoth Water. There is any number of directions, any number of great creatures underneath every surface I see.

From this point, I might start out for everywhere. To dig, to dive. Explore. The room does not lack guidebooks. Promises of authenticity, places to see, to inhabit the city. I could, I'm sure, find my way. Instead, for me, in thirty-six minutes, there will be a call, perfunctory conversation, consequent action. A cab, an elevator, handshakes, more talking, perhaps—if time permits—flowcharts. Then there will be lunch of something; we will assume that it will be stuffed chicken. More talking, handshakes, another cab ride. All of this will start, like clockwork, in, now, thirty-five minutes.

8:11 a.m.—Last night I dreamt I walked through the city, following the inky river. There were, I think, faceless people who stared past me and the streets were lit with colors made smoky and ethereal by fog. My calves ached. I knew only that I was looking for the very tallest building in this place and it was forever popping up just in the distance, then just as quickly vanishing. Soon I was untethered, loose in the streets. Of course, the fog began to spit. I scampered under an awning—a chocolatier, closed for the evening. The smell of the rich sweets and cinnamon in an orange light dizzied me, but nothing compared to the woman in the window sweeping the shop. She looked straight at me and smiled. She was graying at the temples and beautifully icy, a ghost. She went on sweeping and never looked back. I lingered. She must have known that I was there, but the next thing never happened. Everything for me—I can't say why—was shattered in that moment. I knew it was all a dream, and I hurried back, awake, into this room: this inside, that outside.

8:19 a.m.—For the first time since I was a child, I find it impossible to tie a Windsor knot. Too fat, too long, too short. From the mirror I stare back at me, a shiny yellow cloth draped around my neck. Right is left and left is right. I smile and notice the color of my eyes. I take the tie from around my neck and stuff it into my back pocket.

8:27 a.m.—Eighteen minutes. My kingdom—tiny and timed as it may be—for a delusion, a dream. For a sprite to leap across the wide expanse of the unmade bed and crash through the plate glass window. Instead, I can only sit and imagine what has happened in that room across the way, its light still on and unnecessary. Perhaps there was a man and a woman—Swedes, perfunctorily aberrant. There is an ancient camera and they take turns under the drop cloth. Unnatural poses: the rigid crook of an arm and a blank gaze off into the distance. There could be a backdrop—neutral blue—and the resultant photos litter the floor. Images on top of images, staring straight up, unblinking, naked.

Closing in on seventeen minutes.

8:33 a.m.—A runaway from Iowa in the Cold Enormous City. Promises of hot food, a warm bed. She has come for the largesse of large environs. She has found it in a tower, intense light shining on her, warm, clean, nothing between her and the lens, nothing between her and the city but a pane of darkish glass.

8:35 a.m.—No—something less salacious: Art School. It is the beauty and purity of form. The artist's objective, sexless eye. Instead of a camera and drop cloth, it is an easel. The subject is an art student herself, talented but raw, in love with her direction. She is from far away—perhaps very far away. The Orient. The artist is her American teacher, a woman with cropped gray hair and thin limbs, who learns from her student's earnest search. The student—her name is Michiko—learns from the way she is left in the room, alone, still posing, while the older woman is off, away, mixing paints. This is beauty, truth. Symbiotic and refreshing, and they spend the night painting and being painted, as the light shifts, as the quality and drama of the room changes entirely.

Now nine minutes.

8:39 a.m.—The icy chocolatier is not sweeping; she was never sweeping. She wields an outsized paint brush. She is painting the world in the shape of a woman. The icy woman is everywhere and everything: a chocolatier, a Swede, a rail-thin Iowan. She is painting all manner of her forms in every shade of chocolate. Edible, indelible. The music of the spheres. This woman awash in the pure orange light of a hot, distant star. Which is to say all stars; every remote possibility exists in the one bright room in this Great City. Six minutes is an eternity. The Universe was created in such a vast swatch of time.

8:44 a.m.—I must decide. Is it Larry and the lobby for me? Will I ease back into the bathroom, pull the tie from my pocket, twist it around my neck, run a brush through my hair and present my presentable self at the appointed place, the appointed time? Will I look forward to the respite of bland stuffed fowl? Or am I hungry and cold, in search of something else? Is my direction altogether different, a tangent, a skewed ricochet into a Great Tower of Experience hovering above a Giant Body of Water harboring God only knows what kind of Monsters? Or is it simple and soft: warm light, the smell of cinnamon?

The alarm clock stares, the numerals blink before me. I haven't moved. I can't. I won't.

My spirit soars.

Notes on an Intercessory Prayer

———ENTRY #1———

It is said that when Mrs. Bhutto died, her brain—cracked free from its bony cocoon*—sprouted wings and flew to the late afternoon sun, not unlike a fat gray moth.

* Initial controversy re: cause of death. Two bullets to the neck? Shrapnel? Official determination: bomb blast + severe head trauma (head slammed into sun roof) = skull fracture.

I can neither confirm nor deny any of it. I was not there.

————ENTRY #2————

WHAT ELSE I WAS NOT THEN AND AM NOT NOW:

— Pakistani.
— Expert in international relations and/or world history.
— Expert. In anything at all.
— Muslim.
— Brown.
— Dissident.
— Harvard-educated.
— Oxford-educated.
— Born of wealth, privilege.
— A beautiful woman.
— Plotting*

---

* Politics = Plotting. Bhutto family no strangers to either.
To date, conspirators unidentified. Etc.

———ENTRY #3———

WHAT I MUST LEARN MORE ABOUT:

India* v. Pakistan re: Kashmir.

---

* On kindred spirits: "I met Mrs. Ghandi in 1972 when I
accompanied my father to Sibla and I remember then I was a teenager,
I was 18 or 19 years old, and I was wearing my first sari and I was
very concerned that I might trip over the sari and it would come undone
in front of all the international photographers. But I saw Mrs. Ghandi
looking at me from under her eye and I think, in a way, she was
reminded of her own relationship with her father."

—1947 – 48
—1965
—1971→E. Pakistan = Bangladesh

Islamist militants in tribal areas on border w/ Afghanistan. Econ piss-
poor (chronic): foreign exchange reserves decline, currency depreci-
ates, current account deficit widens. Graft. Corruption. Etc.*

---

* On the poverty she saw in her youth: "In Pakistan wealth and poverty exist side by side so one always sees it. I would see it all the time in the people who came to our homes. And there was enormous poverty in Larkana. We had to trek to Larkana every winter and spend time there to get to know our people. And when we went with my father the people would be barefoot and their feet would be caked with mud. Their hair would be matted. They were shirtless. They were shoeless. These were my father's words, he would say to me, Look out of the window. Look at the people who are shoeless. These are the people whom you have to help."

Geography:

—Pakistan (size) ≤ CA x 2.

—Frequent earthquakes—esp in N and W.

—Laka→province of Sindh in S of Pakistan

Lore:
—Bhuttos roots traced to Arab conquest of Sindh→712 AD
—B. Bhutto as a little girl.*

---

* On the Goal of a Woman, part I: "I grew up with a firm belief that a woman could have everything."

————Cut-up in class. Stink bombs. Whoopee cushions.
————First girl to wear a paper dress* in school.

---

* [What is a paper dress?]

————Attended boarding school→Convent in Karachi.*

---

* *"I am a bridge of two cultures, two worlds, and two pasts."*

Father PM→1970s→seeks Bomb. Kissinger tries to warn him off. *The people of Pakistan will eat grass in order to acquire the nuclear bomb.* Rigged elections. Sentenced to death. Guards will not let her embrace him at the end. Three days after the execution, she is allowed to leave prison and pay her last respects.*

---

* On the aftermath of her father's death: *"I used to dream of my father. I would have so many dreams that would recur, and I would say, Oh, but I thought they had killed you. I'm so happy to see that it was wrong and that you're alive. It was really a huge recurrence, and then I would wake up in the mornings and I would be much sadder because I would realize that it had only been a dream. When he first was killed, I could smell his perfume, the scent, it would just come and* go. I feel a little bit dotty repeating these things because they're not very rational, but I had a very strong connection with my father. He was only fifty when he was murdered, and when I turned fifty I realized how young that really is."

———————————————

[Three days: Mary(both of them)/Jesus. Irony?]*

———————————————

* [Are there Islamic saints?]

———————————————

Etc.

————ENTRY #4————

THE REAL TASK AT HAND (TO BE TAKEN UP LATER IN EARNEST):

Mimi.

Who studied art history at the Sorbonne in her university year abroad.

Who believes that Jackson Pollock is the quintessential American artist. All excess movement. Mindless drips and spatters. Unintended. Regurgitant. What someone forgot to clean up. Bluff and persona and nothing more. These are American qualities, I agree. And I reserve judgment on the relative merits of Mr. Pollock's creative output. Mimi would know; I would not. It is her training.

I do know that, though she prefers not to encounter a mess—she is averse to pungent smells, loud noises—, Mimi considers herself to be a full-fledged Citizen of the World. In every respect. This tints her view of many things. America not least. Not least me. That she is possessed of this incongruity, this small but significant lack of self awareness, does not make her a bad person. In fact, she has a great many commendable qualities.*

---

* She has, for instance, an excellent singing voice. Also she knows everything about everything. Then there is the fact that her teeth are perfectly straight, profoundly white. Her intrinsic, unperfumed scent is sweet, powdery. The nape of her neck. Her soft bottom lip. Etc.

---

†

I, on the other hand, am a lifelong creature of the provinces, simple
and gray in both form and function. Like me, my city makes only
a faint glow in a dim, unpeopled American quadrant. Our own
Sindh province. Tribes along the border. Clerics—corrupt and/or
messianic.

At this point, if you are like Mimi, you will raise your brow at me
and make the noise you make at the base of your throat when you
wish to discount me as a harmless dun-colored bore who draws out
parallels, proofs, equations, conclusions that are not borne out in the
phenomenal world. And then you will go on sipping your oolong
tea. How could I possibly know? Where on earth have I ever been?

RY #5——

FIFTY-ONE PLACES WHERE I HAVE NEVER BEEN:

1. Athens
2. Bangalore
3. Beijing
4. Bombay/Mumbai
5. Boston
6. Budapest
7. Buenos Aires
8. Cairo
9. Calcutta
10. Canada
11. Cape Town
12. Ceylon/Sri Lanka
13. Constantinople
14. Cuba
15. Dakar
16. Delhi
17. Dubai
18. Florence
19. Gaza
20. the Grand Canyon
21. Istanbul
22. Kuala Lumpur
23. La Paz
24. Lahore
25. London
26. Los Angeles
27. Madrid

28. Marrakesh
29. Mexico City
30. the Moon
31. Morocco
32. Moscow
33. Myanmar/Burma
34. New York
35. Oslo
36. Port au Prince
37. Prague
38. Reykjavik
39. Rome
40. San Francisco
41. Shanghai
42. Sierra Leone
43. South Dakota
44. Stockholm
45. Sydney
46. Tangiers
47. Tegucigalpa
48. Tehran
49. Tokyo
50. Tripoli
51. Etc.

——ENTRY #6——

DIRECT ADDRESS REGARDING THE NATURE OF BEAUTY IN THE
HUMAN ANIMAL:

Dearest Mrs. Bhutto,
Allow me if you will to set the scene in the present moment. (This is
presumptuous: from your current vantage—that of Formless Infin-
itude—I feel sure you are fully capable of "setting the scene" yourself.) I am not an extraordinary man. I take simple pleasures. One of
them is to sit in a café, sip a sweet, warm something, take up space
in a room full of other people. There are 1.5 interesting cafés in the
midsized provincial American city where I live. I frequent them—
the wholly interesting one somewhat more often than the partly
interesting one—because I know that they will fail soon enough
and I do not want to bear whatever small but statistically significant
percentage of guilt that would be mine if I did not frequent them.

I suspect this is something—a burden?—you know/knew all too
well. Strange as it sounds, the inevitable failure of too-few cafés in a
provincial American city is made of the same stuff as the claw-and-
tooth struggle toward modernity in a country that clings to the sheer
face of its rocky past. (This is precisely the sort of hypothesis I have
learned not to float in the presence of Mimi. She is capable of letting
loose the sharpest of barbed sighs. For all her incense and supple
yoga-pose grace, her equipoise is an easily fractured thing; this too
is something I would not say to her directly.)

Thus: at lunchtime on this particular clear, warm winter day,
there are between 29 and 43 patrons in the one wholly interesting
café in the wholly ordinary city where I live. One of the things that
makes me a wholly ordinary man—if, indeed, "not extraordinary" =
ordinary—is that I, without thinking much about it, take measure of

the women in the room. There are, in the ebb and flow of a lunch-time rush, an average of 2.5-4.25 beautiful women. This floating range of statistical probabilities allows for a series of unpredictable variables and intangibles, as is always only appropriate whenever we endeavor to understand what drives the human animal. The number of our desires is never exact, never whole, never wholly clean.

First, I am aware that this quick and particular calculation might create the impression that I am somehow not ordinary at all. Ordinary men, the argument goes, do not make such a calculus of lust or desire or whatever it is a man does vis-à-vis "beauty." To a degree, I take the point. However, I would argue that the calculation is actually quite ancient and hardwired. It is only when we choose to turn it into a number—more accurately, a *fraction*—as opposed to a poem and/or a portrait and/or an advertisement that it becomes noteworthy and somehow aberrant.

Second, I am aware that my conception of beauty is less solid and sure than it once was: it is now (if you'll allow the imperfect metaphor) a slow-moving magma, the kind that bubbles and belches just under the surface of a dormant hole in the ground, threatening at all times to spill out upon the unwitting city in the valley below, and yet, in fact, rarely ever boiling over to make itself known.

All metaphors are, of course, imperfect.

——ENTRY #7——

SELECTED OTHER CONTEMPORARY EMBODIMENTS OF THE DIVINE
FEMININE:

—Diana, Princess of Wales (Deceased)
—the German Tennis Player Steffi Graf (Retired)
—the former Prime Minister of Great Britain Margaret Thatcher
(Deceased?)
—the Indian/American Fiction Writer Jhumpa Lahiri
—the English Novelist Zadie Smith
—the former American Press Secretary Dee Dee Myers
—the American Political Blogger/Journalist Ana Marie Cox
—the American Singer/Songwriter Ani DiFranco
—the American Semi-Expatriate Pop Icon Madonna ("Our Lady")
—the American Political Commentator Cokie Roberts
—the Lebanese/Jordanian/Mexican Film Actress Salma Hayek
—the Irish Singer/Songwriter and Provocateur Sinéad O'Connor
—Queen Noor of Jordan
—the American Basketball Player Sue Bird
—the former American Secretary of State, former Junior Senator of
New York, and former First Lady Hillary Rodham Clinton
—the Jamaican Singer/Songwriter, Model, and Film Actress Grace
Jones
—the American Basketball Coach Pat Summitt
—Etc.

————ENTRY #8————

DIRECT ADDRESS REGARDING WHAT I AM UP TO, INCLUDING
DISCLAIMERS (WHY I AM FULLY AWARE IT IS TOO LATE FOR
INTERVENTION, WHY THE FAULT IS, OF COURSE, ALL MINE, ETC.)

PART II:

In any event, Dearest Mrs. Bhutto—

This is the best I can manage in the way of —patronage?—
noblesse oblige?—self-preservation and/or—indulgence and/or
conspicuous consumption: in a probably misguided and very likely
vain attempt to keep my favorite café in business, I sometimes order
the most expensive item on the menu, which is oddly enough a
mixed green salad. The premium reflects not the degree to which the
food does the most primitive (and vital) thing food can do—fill an
empty place in the body that is meant to be filled—but the degree to
which these ingredients (several of the more nutritional varieties of
lettuce/leafy greens [arugula, Romaine, Boston, baby spinach, etc.];
blueberries and strawberries; walnuts, lightly roasted; a clean, white
clump of organic goat cheese; a sensible and unobtrusive homemade
vinaigrette, on the side) might extend the length (by which I mean
number) of one's days. It is a mark of privilege to choose such forth-
coming residual hunger. Science now says it is healthier for us to be
a little bit empty. So it costs more. I pay the premium to keep myself
and the café empty and alive. Moral value accrues in the smallest
transactions: what you put in your mouth; what you pay for; the
company you keep.

To wit—

Two tables over, a woman wolfs a pimento cheese sandwich.
Between hunched-over, even furtive, bites of a dill spear.

A man makes a show of trading the one rickety wooden chair at the table next to mine for a rickety metal one in the far corner of the café. He sits facing the window, the impossibly bright blue day. He opens his *New York Times* and waits—*

---

* [Please understand: what I am concerned with here is conveying my own paltry experience of the inexorable rise-and-fall, inhale-exhale on the fringes of what some regard as the Greatest Civilization on Earth. So that you may better acquaint yourself with my—as it were—"plight" and thereby intercede, if you choose to, somewhat more three-dimensionally.]

—for his salad, which comes soon enough, borne by a ludicrously pretty young man with curly dark hair and three days growth of stubble. A scruffy Dionysus in a tight green thrift-store soccer jersey. The man in the metal chair assures Dionysus that everything is as he expects. When their exchange is over and he is alone again, the man in the metal chair takes great care to scoop the clot of goat cheese into his cupped palm. He carries it like a trembling egg to the trash bin then returns to his pile of greens, licking his palm all the way.

†

PART III:

Therefore, Dearest Mrs. Bhutto—

It is quite possible (likely) that a single and unassailable truth will always form an obstruction between us, and that is my history as a run-of-the-mill Caucasoid American man; in particular, the fact that I was—(I will not admit that I still *am*—it is only partway true, in the way that a person can never be sure he is rid of cancer, even if it has been in remission for years—and besides it would confirm Mimi's worst fears about me)—an ersatz Romantic. The pale and humorless sort of man who spent his suburban American youth dizzied by the uncanny significance—Truth, Authenticity, Insight—contained in the early, wry, semi-comedic dramas ("dramedies") of the earnest American Film Actor John Cusack.

I only mention it because I suspect that whatever it is I want from you, Mrs. Bhutto—if I can, in fact, be said to want something from you—would require not just sympathy but real *empathy*. A mile in my moccasins, as it were. But I must also admit—and this is a real concern—that even I have trouble empathizing with myself.*

---

* [Mimi would name this sentiment as pathetic, self-serving. It would be disingenuous of me if I did not cede the point.]

I mention it in the spirit of full (if unnecessary) disclosure: I am not made of the same stuff—Spirit—as you.*

---

* On her imprisonment after her father's execution: "It *was very difficult. There were cockroaches and flies. Very bad sanitation. I had nobody to talk to and the loneliness was enormous. I remember it was very cold in the winters, it was very hot in the summers. Mosquitoes and flies would not let you sleep. So the sustenance that I got was from my connection to God.*"

——ENTRY #9——

A HYPOTHETICAL: WHAT I WOULD PRAY FOR IF I WAS THE EAR-
NEST AMERICAN FILM ACTOR JOHN CUSACK (OR SOME REASON-
ABLE FACSIMILE THEREOF):

—The proper sequence of words—earnest, unadorned, "real"—
written in ball point pen (blue) on plain lined paper, folded many
times, and delivered surreptitiously to a doe-eyed young woman
who is perfectly unaware that she is beautiful; who is earnest,
unadorned, "real;" who is inclined to "make a difference" in the
world; who is a better, happier, smarter person than I could ever
hope to be. It will be these right—earnest, unadorned, "real"—
words that will somehow bridge the wide natural gulf between us.
—Some idiosyncratic collage of pop music cobbled together using
the appropriate technology of the age, designed to produce this same
bridging (earnest, unadorned, etc) effect.

—…which is to say I would pray for True Love, however improbable—which is to say I would pray for the Quintessential American
Indulgence.*

---

* On Love v. Respect in marriage: "In love marriages,
love comes first and then goes. But in an arranged
marriage, respect comes first and then love grows. I
was always puzzled when people said, *As a modern woman
how could you have an arranged marriage?* But then I realized
that for most people in the West, *arranged* meant *forced*,
and mine was not a forced marriage."

—Throughout the ordeal, I would be blissfully ignorant of the Essential Nature of a Woman, any woman*—

---

* On the goal of a woman, part II: *"We grow up in a particular tradition and then we are exposed to ideas of modernity. We try to combine both together to fashion our own identities. My mother herself was a captain in Pakistan's guards. She was the first person in Karachi who was a lady to drive a car, and this was very shocking to most people, that a lady should be driving a car. And yet my mother was brought up to believe that the goal of a woman was to get married, to have a good husband, to get a good home, and to rear good children. So my mother was simply horrified at the prospect that my father wanted to send me to university and I'd be an old maid by the time I returned in my mid-twenties and nobody would want to marry me... Every time I came back for the summer, my mother would try to arrange my marriage."*

— precisely because I would have accepted the fabrication that there is, in fact, such a thing as the Essential Nature of a Woman, any woman.*

---

* On the goal of a woman, part III: *"It is interesting that the person who ensured that I would break loose of the constraints of my culture and gender was not a woman but a man."*

————ENTRY #10————

DIRECT ADDRESS REGARDING WHAT I AM NOT ASKING FOR AND
WHAT I AM

PART IV:

Therefore—

What I am not asking for and what I am:
    I am not asking for a secret. I am not asking to understand. I am
not asking for peace, for myself or anyone else. I am not even asking
to be a better person or to better my circumstances. What I want
is to trade in my history. Not forever or even for very long. But for
some small but measurable period of time, I want to be empty and
for you to fill me full of something like self-contained bravery, even
as I wade back into the Failed State I and the person(s) closest to me
have built.

——ENTRY #11——

THE REAL TASK AT HAND: A TIMELINE (PART I):

—Boy meets girl in café. A mid-sized American city in the unsuspecting world. Girl: tight-cropped black ringlets. Unblemished skin, milk-white. Excellent singing voice. Etc. Boy: pensive. Asymmetrical in form, function, spirit. What he lacks in symmetry, he makes up for in a conspicuous lack of guile. This commends him to her, though there is a good chance she would never admit it.

—Boy is not a boy at all. He is not quite old enough to be her father but all the same he is too old for her. There is an entire summer of stolen moments. Time when no one in the waking world occupies the same universe as these two star-crossed (to borrow a term from antiquity, its outsized attachment to Romance, its romanticization of Sadness) lovers.

—Girl goes to Paris, City of Lights. She learns to talk about Art and to smoke cigarettes and to make love without even a hint of embarrassment. *I'm not just someone's daughter anymore.*

Upon her return, for six months, a year, it is as if their stolen summer never happened. She dates young men, boys, really, who do not yet suffer the ignominy of hair in the wrong spots, etc. They are something like Greek statues, etc. And yet. To paraphrase the American Stand-up Comedian and Film Actor Eddie Murphy, these well-formed young men are still at the stage in their conjugal lives when, somewhere just beneath the veneer of lust and dexterous Primal Agency, they are astonished at their good fortune to be *en flagrante* with anyone,* much less someone who is at least as well-formed (likely moreso) as they are.

---

* *"[They] be surprised [they] be fuckin'."*—E. Murphy

—Thus: a hair's breadth opening. He bides his time—

———ENTRY #12———

DIRECT ADDRESS REGARDING THAT WHICH LINKS PAST, PRESENT, FUTURE:

And then there's this, Dearest Mrs. Bhutto—

Word is Your Stunning Niece the Poet has caught the eye of the American Film Actor George Clooney. Himself the Stunning Nephew of Someone Famous. In his case, Rosemary Clooney. *C'mon a my house a my house I'm gonna give you candy.* Your Stunning Niece the Poet is half Our Film Actor's age but we have begun the Era of Timelessness— of decades sloughed off by miracle rubs, ointments, procedures, food, drink, herbs. What the two of them share is the way Stunning People are forced to take themselves quite seriously. How grave is your Niece's countenance. Grave because the way she looks—something from a magazine, a billboard—something airbrushed and not entirely corporeal—something like a dream contained in a shell of smooth dusky skin—it is something she must either wield or ignore. Or worse: she must strike some impossible balance between the two.

None of this, I know for sure, is news to you. Your Stunning Niece the Poet does not strike the fancy of Our Handsome Moviestar because she came upon her grave beauty by accident. It was preordained by the Limitless Poetry at the Beginning of the Universe—*and the Earth was formless and void and the Spirit moved over the surface of the waters*— crackling with the promise of what we now recognize as Light, Heat, Motion, a current of colors. Or you could simply call it heredity. Regardless. There is something of all of this in the both of you.

Thus, a confession—

I am tempted to believe there is something of both of you in *all of us*, though this hypothesis is not measurable, not provable, very nearly theoretical. Or worse: merely a matter of faith, what most cynics dismiss as bald-faced *superstition*. Etc.

——ENTRY #13——

THE REAL TASK AT HAND: ABSTRACTED INTERMITTENT GESTURES,
MOMENTS; WITH WHITE SPACE AND NO SMALL MEASURE OF
INARTICULATION:

I have a black-and-white photograph of Mimi as a little girl. She is
smiling with her eyes closed and her hair is wet. The picture shows
only her face—not where she is or who she's with—so I don't know
(and she doesn't remember) why her hair is wet. Her unsullied skin
glistens. This is not a smile I have ever known her to make in the
time and space we've shared. I am tempted to believe it is only make-
believe, to invent the hot summer day and the thick smell of some
fragrant blossom(s) and/or just-cut grass moving in a warm mass to
occupy all the air around her, everything *around* the air around her. A
protective enclosure of Careless Summer. And the cool, clear water
from the hose. Her house in the near suburbs, when the American
suburbs were still a possible source of goodness in the world, still
unquestioned, still earnest and "real," if not unadorned. The promise
of it. Of some purple-sweet iced treat. Of her—Mimi—this little
girl—smiling in the bright hot American summertime.

†

Once, on an unseasonably warm day, during a winter like this one,
while she napped on the unmade bed, I placed that very photo on
the lumpy pillow by her face. Her face now inches away from the
face she used to have, if the photographic evidence is to be trusted.

Point A—Point B.*

---

* *"I am a bridge of two cultures, two worlds, and two pasts."*

How One Gets From There to Here.*

---

* Ibid.

Incremental Perturbations; conflict, climax; a causally related
sequence of events.*

---

* Ibid.

This necessary amnesia: translating what happened a long time ago to the intuitive apparatus of dreams. Or prayers. What tools a young woman uses to know her future, to keep her hopes up, to keep her options open, to believe that she will, in fact, get everything she's ever wanted in this world.

————ENTRY #14————

Hail Mary, full of grace,
the Lord is with thee;
blessed art thou amongst women,
and blessed is the fruit of thy womb, Jesus.
Holy Mary, Mother of God,
pray for us sinners,
now and at the hour of our death. Amen.

——ENTRY #15——

THE PROBLEM OF PRAYER:

What I am praying for:

Some Other Intelligence—Presence—Intelligent Presence.

The one I have in me, such as it is, cannot grasp the sum total sequence of my experience. The small life I have lived. Smaller than I could have ever imagined.

Life in fits and starts, in (and of) fractions.

The difference between what I want and what I should have.

——ENTRY #16——

THE REAL TASK AT HAND: A TIMELINE (PART II):

—Boy (who is not really a boy) meets Girl (who is no longer a girl) in a café. She is studying what passes for a local avant-garde newsweekly, sipping her oolong tea. She picks the berries from a morning bowl of assorted fruit, eats them one by one, almost as an afterthought. Unintended and (therefore?) exquisite grace.

—Boy, pained, interrupts; her face softens into what he interprets as a genuine smile.

—The subsequent/requisite *how are you, you look well, so do you, sit down, I can't stay I wish I could, so excellent to see you, you look well, so do you, I wish I could stay.* Etc.

—In the distracted aftermath, as they try in vain to regain their footing on the respective paths they were traveling (mediocre newsweeklies; berries; grace; oolong tea; a beloved café on a Saturday morning; the plain and ancient smell of eggs cooking in a cast-iron skillet somewhere in the kitchen; the contented relief associated with indefinite solitude in this bright blue world of simple, articulate smells and tastes, with being wholly unattached to any particular fate, to any of the world's particular Others) they both wonder if the on-again-off-again arrangement between them is somehow on again. Just as they both know it can't last.

—"Love comes first and then goes." Etc.

Life in fits and starts, in (and of) fractions.

What we want. What we should have.

What we want

What we should have

†

Proof:

Whereas—
—Human beings, it has been observed, form unions, attachments.
This is an intuitive skill.
—The disparate contemplative traditions are loath to promise per-
manence of forms.
—Disintegration, in its various forms, is the single fact said traditions
can agree upon.

Prove:
    That the faith and fortitude to turn back, still once more, to the
failed state of one's own making—to do so with love and abandon—
falls within the realm of acceptable human endeavor:

————Military vehicles swarm the tarmac. A commercial airliner
taxis in to the terminal;
————House arrest, broken intermittently by a series of forays into
the dusty, broken
countryside;
————Crowds and tumult;
————The fiction of precautionary measures;
————The predictable sequence of near misses—bombs, etc. Dozens
dead on the periphery;
————Then, in time, the one swift blast that shatters the mind into
something like infinity.

Come to Jesus

From the very start, Jesus would not take root in me. The last time I ever went to Sunday school, I was eight and Mrs. Cantrell was up there telling us about Moses and the tablets. I had a question about "Thou shalt have no other gods before me." Seemed to me that proved for sure there *were* other gods and God Jehovah was afraid we would two-time him. Mrs. Cantrell—who, up to that point, gave me a little flutter every time she walked by and I smelled her Chanel No. 5—came at me like I had sprouted horns. She had an evil look and she made me say that commandment two hundred and fifty times, right then and there, with everybody listening. I got to 178 and, for some reason, I started with the dry heaves. Nerves, I guess. Mrs. Cantrell slapped me so hard for stopping, her hair came partway undone.

Momma had people come by to talk to me at various times from then on. Easter was a popular time for that sort of thing. That is because it was spring and Momma felt like the warming air and ground would melt my heart for the resurrected Jesus. It never really did, though sometimes I made whoever it was feel like they had made some headway, just to be polite. I remember my cousin Alfred who was a sophomore up at the Bible college, studying to be a preacher himself, telling me one spring in my junior year of high school, "You'll make it, Bobby. Jesus don't mind questioning souls." But I knew Alfred did not know his dick from a biscuit, so I just let him talk.

†

Up until Jamie's freshman year, I dated Bonnie Stevens who had a pug nose and great big tits and she would let you touch her on the outside of her panties but not on the inside. She was nice and good to talk to and she did not say things to embarrass you when you were with your friends. But when Jamie came to school, Bonnie became the second prettiest girl in school, and the quarterback in my high school—which I was—dates the prettiest girl. That is how things are. Everybody knows it.

Jamie was beyond her years. She was tall and lean and she carried herself like she was prom queen on the very first day of school. She smiled easy and she was smarter than everybody else and her hair was a shiny cinnamon color. There was no mystery about it, especially between Jamie and me. The second day after school started, she just walked up to my car after football practice and asked for a ride home. That was it. Things start that way. I told Bonnie over Sonic milkshakes and she called me a pervert and cried and asked me who she was going to marry when the whole damn county was full of water heads and petty criminals. I do not remember what I said.

Before we had even kissed, Jamie told me about a boy, Stevie McIntosh, who was staring at her in homeroom and making her feel nervous. Stevie was just a little kid, scrawny with something wrong with his legs that made him run funny. Still, when we were all out at Donald Lee's barn drinking beer one Friday night, I made sure Stevie got invited so I could dangle him from the hayloft by his legs and not let him down until he said he would leave Jamie alone. Me and Jamie were dating after that. I remember the look she gave me when I told her what I had done. She was in love and a little scared at the same time. She was not afraid of what I might do, to her or anybody else. She could handle that. She was afraid right then and there of what might happen to somebody as nasty and brutish as me.

†

Jamie always feared God and told me so.

"Bobby Watkins," she would say, "God's in everything." She said that all the time. Lots of times she would say something to that effect right before she kissed me sweetly on the cheek, took my hand from whatever soft, warm place it had found on her angelic form, and said she was ready for me to take her home. Then one night—by this time I had graduated from school and was working for the highway department—she did not take my hand away.

"Bobby," she said. "You believe me when I say God's everywhere, don't you?" She looked up into my face and I knew to nod. She smiled, knowing what was going to happen next, knowing that I did not know. She unzipped me and I leaned back into the headrest to give her room. She fluttered her tongue across the tip of it, which is a tender place. It nearly hurt. What it did was ache, and ache, it turns out, is good.

"God doesn't get in the way of true love, Bobby."

Fuck. Sweet Jesus, is what I shouted inside my head.

But all I ever said out loud was yes. More than once. And I shuddered and said her name. Over and over again. Then, after a while, she slipped off her shorts and got on top of me. Her hair fell beautiful down her shoulders, into her face, wild. There was the mild slap of us, which embarrassed me, and her muttering softly in between very wet kisses, which did not, and I cannot ever tell you what something like that is like, to live through, to remember it for the rest of your days.

†

She was pregnant by the next April and we got married that June, on Jamie's eighteenth birthday, two days before her high school graduation. Alfred did the ceremony. Momma and Daddy loved her, even though we got into trouble the way we did, because she was repentant and churchgoing and she loved me and Ella. They thought she might be the one to turn me around. Her parents let on like they did not hate me too much, I guess because at least I had a job.

For the first few years, we would all three get dressed up—me, Jamie, and Ella—and drive over to Momma's to pick them up. Then we would go to the church and I would help herd everybody in. Once we were at our regular pew, I clasped my hands in front of me and just let my mind wander. I would think about whatever highway work I had coming up or I would think about football or something stupid like that. Never God, though. Jamie's best friend, Marlene, sometimes sat with us. Marlene would look out the window, hit my knee and giggle when I nodded off. She would whisper under her breath when the service was over, "Holy shitfire," she would say, "I need a beer." I liked Marlene.

After church, we had afternoon dinner at Momma's, sat in the living room for just long enough, then went back to our little trailer, which was down off Highway 43, back in among the pines. It was rickety and worn out, but it was cheap, and the job I had at the time did not pay enough for anything else. Usually, Jamie's parents would be waiting for us—they did not live but a mile away—and we visited until the sun went down. They loved Ella, spoiled her with cookies and treats and presents, and then they would sneak some money to Jamie so she could have nice things. I did not mind. I was glad for her to have nice things. Sometimes, if Ella got to clinging on her Grandma and wanted to spend the night, Marlene would come over to our place after and we would talk and drink beer.

"Darla Collins is with a black guy down in Washington County." Marlene always knew who was with a black guy somewhere.

"She's that way," Jamie might say.

Then I might say that it was not any big thing, half believing it because of the beer, and they would laugh at me.

"So you wouldn't care if Jamie took up with a black guy?"

"That ain't the point, Marlene. I don't want her taking up with anybody."

"You're saying it wouldn't be worse if it was a black guy?"

"I'm saying that's a stupid example."

And then Jamie would come over and sit on my lap and kiss my forehead and my nose and tell me, "Baby, don't you worry. If I take up with anybody, it'll be Marlene."

After Marlene was finally gone, Jamie and I would tear the house up with our drunken, stumbling congress. Sometimes I would have to put my hand over Jamie's mouth—which could get strangely, gloriously foul in those moments—for fear that her parents would hear us way on down the road.

†

The trouble was, Ella started to be old enough to talk and ask questions. She is sharp. She got that from Jamie. Jamie had been on me about talking right to her, making sure the child was properly God-fearing. I told her I was for it, but really I was not. Or I guess I did not care, which is just about the same thing as being against it. Funny how just when everything is finally getting calm and it seems pretty clear everything is going to be all right, one little thing can turn it back the other way. We had moved out of that trailer and, with some help from our parents, we bought a tiny little house. With Ella starting preschool, Jamie was starting to think about some classes at the junior college over in Monroeville.

Problem was Jamie was fairly certain by now that I was headed for bad ends. It was not any one thing that made me an unbeliever in her eyes, and she still loved me as far as I could tell. But, for one thing, I had made it a habit to avoid church. Usually I had a real excuse. There was work to do on the house that I could not do any other time. The tiny little back porch was rotten so I had to tear that up and build a new one, only this time bigger and better. It was always something.

Jamie could let herself ignore that, I suppose. It was Ella's questions. She was full of them and not shy about asking. Somehow she bounced back and forth between me and Jamie, comparing answers like some kind of city lawyer, digging out the inconsistencies and making us account for them. And I just kept answering them wrong.

"Where does God live?" Ella asked.

"God don't live anywhere."

"Momma says He lives in everybody's heart."

"Oh."

"That's not what you said," she reminded me. "You said he don't live anywhere."

"I was wrong, I guess."

"How come?"

"I don't know."

"How come you don't know?"

"Go be with your Momma, okay?"

"Momma says you don't think like everybody else about things," she told me.

"Baby, don't start up with that again. I told you."

"But I don't know why."

"Why, what?"

"Why you don't like God."

"I like God fine."

"That's not what Momma says."

And so it would go.

†

Marlene moved to Mobile to live with her sickly aunt. Right after she got down there, she turned to Jesus and dating women, though nobody could tell which came first. The former was more of a surprise than the latter to most of us who knew her. She had only dated scrawny little Billy Adgate in high school, and that was in tenth grade. She said Billy gagged whenever they tried to kiss with any kind of vigor, so it stands to reason she did not like it much. From then, she mostly just attached herself to Jamie's hip, over at our place all the time, just being a part of things, but that did not bother me.

It did not even bother me to hear she turned gay—or that she finally admitted it. Mobile could do that to you. I was more taken aback by her conversion to righteousness.

"But she hated church," I said to Jamie.

"That's God's way," she said. And she looked at me for a long time.

"What?" I asked her.

"Nothing."

"It's just damn strange, is all." That is all I could think to say.

Not long after that Marlene came up for a visit. That is what they told me, anyway. Turns out, they were up to something. It was just like any other early spring day. Jamie had made my lunch, kissed me quick on the cheek, and headed over to drop Ella off at preschool while she went to classes in Monroeville. "See you tonight," she told me. "Marlene's coming." I nodded and gave Ella a kiss. She laughed because I had not shaved and the stubble tickled her chin. I worked, got hot in the sun, ate my lunch, laughed real hard with a big black guy named Maurice about something I cannot really remember, and I worked some more. Then it was time to go home. Only there was not any home when I got there. It was there, but it was dark and cold and it did not smell like dinner. There was a cut-out newspaper ad taped to the kitchen counter, a man, sweaty in the face and pointing out at me, full of conviction: *Are You Ready for the Rapture?* Underneath, in Jamie's perfect cursive:

> *Marlene says it's for your own good and if you don't she can take your place easy.*
>
> > Love, Us.

†

I go to the damn thing. What choice do I have? On the drive up, I start to think maybe I am adrift, maybe I have been for a long time. Yes, for goddamn sure, I am. It starts to feel as if my whole paltry life has been leading up to this night. Or maybe I just want it to feel that way. The civic center is a mess, what with all the buses, and there is no place to park. Finally, I park the truck in an alley and I am too expectant to be worried about it. In no time, I am ushered to a seat in the very back by some Mexican guy with a flashlight. There is a little man down there—maybe the man from the newspaper—and he is dressed all in white. He is full of something: energy, spirit, God, shit. Maybe all of it. Soon enough, they are lining up to be saved. Even though I start down there as quick as I know to do it, it is a long way from the very top of the arena down to the floor. There is a line of people in front of me and I begin to worry that I will not make it to the stage. Meanwhile, the lights are down low and there is a long, hypnotic session of singing and hosannas, ending with minutes on end of "Hallelujah." All real slow and soft. Finally I feel dizzy enough that if I had never seen the carnival man hypnotize people and make them cluck like chickens, I might think the Spirit was swirling around me, waiting to dive in at the right opportunity. I try to count the people in front of me, but lose track when the number gets to be over a hundred.

"Son," says the woman in front of me. She has on a neck brace and all manner of amulets in the form of the Savior. "You look like you're in trouble."

I kind of nod my head. I thought everybody who got in line was in some form of trouble. That is the point, after all. I do not say that, though. I just say "Yes, ma'am."

"You step on in front of me," she says. "I been saved at one of these in Ft. Worth in 1988. I just mainly got a bad crick in the neck now."

Up there ahead of me, the children are not exactly buying it. One kid says he does not want to be saved by Jesus today—says it outright, loud, into the microphone. Wants his help on a test, though. The Man does not bother to lay hands on him. Nor does he try to lay hands on the very little kids—Grace and Noah—whose parents brought them all the way over from Little Rock, Arkansas. The parents complained of some malady or another and he made short order of shooting them down with his healing powers. The kids are left standing, kind of scared, not knowing what they are supposed to do. The Man just chuckles, says something about how wonderful it is that they have names such as they do.

I get to the stairs and I can feel the hot, white light. There is a man moving down the line. He is the one who asks you what is wrong with you. Mostly it is fibromyalgia, asthma, mysterious lumps. One lady tells him she had been to The Man before, got healed, and a Jewish doctor told her it was nonsense. They laugh together, like the world is full of silly Jew doctors who do not know shit. Then he gets to me.

"My wife ran off with a lesbian," I tell him.

He gets wide in the eyes.

"Sort of," I say. "We're all friends. I'm pretty sure she's coming back."

He has got this little pad he's supposed to write things down on but he is not writing.

"The real problem is—" but I draw a blank.

†

While I wait for the Rapture, I think about Jamie and how she is a perfect breath of air. I wonder how these things come to a person, out of nowhere. How one soul—smart and beautiful and God-fearing—is drawn to another who works with his body out in the sun, somebody who has to feel something in his hand to know it for sure. Jamie takes classes—she wants to be a schoolteacher and she will be a good one—and the books she reads are thick as a brick. History. English. Biology. I am not stupid. I know what is in those books, and when we talk about something that interests her—maybe Napoleon or amoebas—we can talk for a long time, with Ella asking sweet, simple questions and me or Jamie—mostly Jamie—answering them. I am fine as long as there are answers to the questions. I do not mess that kind of thing up.

I get snapped out of my thoughts by the choir. They are singing and everybody starts clapping their hands. The people in front of me have disappointed looks on their faces. I look for The Man but he's gone. The stage sorely misses his presence. This close, I can see all the duct tape that holds the gray carpet together. The lights in the arena come up. The music stops and only the hum of the crowd hangs in the air. The dark is gone and it feels like I can see every single face staring up at me. I am four people away from the stair to the stage. Less than twenty souls in between mine and eternal salvation.

Before I can get too sad about that, here comes a posse of The Man's assistants. They are all in stiff suits. They fan out into the crowd, talking, hugging, smiling. They hunch over wheelchairs, take somebody's nubby wrist in their hands as a salutation. Two of them peel off and starting working the line. One of them, a big man with a hairy neck and large black eyes, gets behind the people in line, the other—a blond-headed man who looks like he has never had to shave a day in his life—talks to each person softly, takes their hands in his and prays. At first he is real quiet about it, but then he gets worked up. The first soul belongs to a thin little black woman who has been quivering the whole time she has been in line. Her eyes are rheumy and she does not look like she is aware of what is going on around her. The blond-headed man starts chanting something and then he shoves his open palm firmly into her chest. She falls out, into the big, dark man's arms. They move down the line this way. I lose track of what happens to the people as they get pushed into salvation. As they approach me, I hear people talking as they file out to the exits. They are not bothered at all by all this pushing and falling. A woman, long-haired and pretty, says, "This evening was so wonderful—just imagine what heaven must be like."

So I imagine what heaven must be like. In my heaven, there are no silver clouds or folks with wings. In my heaven, there is mud and water and the smell of the woods. There is Jamie and there is Ella and maybe even Marlene. Mrs. Cantrell's perfume gets to be there, but not the woman herself. There are two-by-fours in my heaven. In my heaven, I get to keep my callused hands.

When the two men reach me, put their soft, smooth hands upon me, I make up my mind. The blond man chants and I close my eyes. As I fall back, I mumble something to God Almighty, that He take up firm and conspicuous residence within me simply because my wife will be sad if he does not. And she does not deserve to be sad. She should just be happy. Always. The big man catches me in his meaty hands. And then I wait, patient, for a time when I can open my eyes and look up into my Jamie's smiling face again, as if I really am new to the world, as if my march to Bliss will be sure-footed, steady. Straight and smooth as some hot, black highway.

Hope, Faith, and Love

The Machinist

Our father—the Father of us All—stands dumb in the garage, hands slick and black with grease. It is October. The sky is a bright, hurtful blue. Our father believes the car is sick, that its sickness carries over into us. *I'm going to see about that car,* he tells Mother, and he does. We just eat our eggs as noises from the garage spill into the house: curses, epithets, good metal clanging bad. Mother tsk-tsks and wipes her hair from her eyes. She lights a cigarette and, when the littlest declares himself full, she spoons his scrambled into her mouth in two quick motions. *Get on outside,* she tells us, *play. It's Saturday.* Saturdays are for playing, so we do. We climb high in the One Pale Sycamore Tree so that we might inhabit the bright blue sky. That close to the sun, it is warm, and with all of us in the tree, it fairly buckles from our weight. We are our own planet, spinning, teeming. There is no telling what Cosmos we occupy. Only occasionally is our orbit interrupted with a muffled tink-tink-tink or some other small ratchet sound from inside the garage. Then, finally, with the sun at the very top of the sky, the Automatic Door starts its slow groan. Up it goes, letting light pour into our black garage. Out the rusty Green Gremlin creeps, our father at the wheel, signaling a left turn out the drive and puttering hesitantly down the street, a plume of black smoke in His wake.

The Excavators

On days when Mother wears her Sad Bonnet and the Hoop Skirt with the Giant Red Bow in the back, those of us with an aversion to her mournful ways go out back to the Sandbox. Bonnet days engender in her a powerful listlessness. She floats through the house like an apparition. It is better to be out of doors, under the full watch of the vigilant sun. *Don't get all dirty-kneed,* she calls after us, though that is precisely our endeavor. Our little Box is up against the ratty fence between us and the Neighbors'. From our years of tireless digging, it's a sandless and deep thing, overhead of even the tallest. All us piled in there is a thing to see. Our Father calls it "That Blamed Pauper's Grave Out Back." Once, when he was in his cups and giddy, he came out with a sack of flour, doused us with fistfuls of make-believe lime, to disinfect our make-believe corpses. Mother blurted epithets, mainly for the loss of flour. We didn't pay the dusting any mind. In the Box, we are nothing but dust and plastic shovels and digging. We find there an overpowering state of our own kind of make-believe; nothing wrenches us out. Some folks say digging straight down leads to Hell or, even worse, China and the Yellow Races. Not so: a tunnel down is a tunnel to the very heart of things. There, the air is cool and dark. A grand Silence echoes forth.

The Fisher King

When we are hungry and Mother lolls on the chaise and smokes her cigarettes and won't get up to feed us, we fend for ourselves. When there is a jar of peanut butter, we take spoons to it. If not peanut butter, then crackers and sweet relish. Our Father has bitterer tastes. Afternoons, He comes sweaty and soiled from some work or another, and looks askance at Mother. *You worthless thing,* He whispers under His breath. *You!* she blurts. *You stay out of my sight.* He mumbles some more and heads into the kitchen for sustenance. His favorite is to take a can of oil-soaked sardines and slurp them like a seal. We watch Him open the can slow and pinch out the headless, shiny fish one by one. He barely chews; His throat muscles work down chunks. Then the pop of a pop-top. Up the bubbles foam. This He slurps too and disappears into the garage for the evening. Mother says, *Thank heavens for that,* and rests her eyes. Our eyes turn to that tin, the puddle of oil in it, and the gray bits of fish-flesh leftover. Would that the world wouldn't empty itself so easy. We peel off, one of us here, two more there, and so on that way until we all find other things to do with our hunger. All night there's that one empty can sitting alone on the table. In the morning—no one knows how—the tin isn't there. The whole kitchen smells like a womb.

The Songstress

Mother dear pretends she is a girl. She sings her popular songs under her mournful breath. This is a frightening spectacle and Our Father shuts His mouth, afraid of what might be next. We scatter into the basement like mice and pray to heaven that her voice doesn't carry down to us. It doesn't and we are safe until one of the sisters starts in with her humming. Though we tell her, *Don't take after mother if you can help it*, she takes after her. So much so that down there amongst the ducts and the unfinished funk, her voice is mother's confession to us all: children I am too tired to feed anyone much less your hungry horde. I did not ask for this life, dears. I want a slow smoke on a back porch, a man with soft hands. I want to breathe clean again. Go, dears, scatter into the hinterlands and spread the word—I've taught you all I know. Our Father calls down to us. *Come up, come up here, children. Got-dammit, come up.* And we do, all of us save for one— she who started in with the humming. Instead of ascending back into the house proper, she stays, humming, until she dissolves into a solitary sound that haunts the pipes on bitter cold days. Back up in the blaring sunshine of Our Father, not a one of the rest of us makes a noise. Mother passes a plate of Grahams and we nibble. He eyes us over the brim of His coffee cup, then a loud, punctuating slurp.

Baby-Boy

Our Father works in mysterious ways: Mother is with child again.
Perhaps even she doesn't know how it happened. Or perhaps there
is another Universe they visit in the long, dark hours of the night. In
the gestation months, Our Father doesn't look at Mother's bulbous
belly. Mother carries it like a measured weight—like a sack of dry
goods from the store, like something other than herself. When her
water breaks, it spills a salty ocean onto the kitchen floor. *Don't get
your Daddy*, she tells us. *Don't*. Her eyes are bright and wild. She pushes
and pushes. The crown is Crowned—it glimmers gold and shiny and
sharp between her legs. Mother bleeds and breathes and pushes, all
right there on the dirty floor. Baby-Boy saunters out. We field him.
For the first seven years, he talks a blue streak and won't let anybody
touch his bright Crown. Baby-Boy, we learn quickly, can be a both-
ersome sort without any answers. When we ask what He's come to
do, Baby-Boy says, *I'm supposed to do something?* When we come right
out and say it—*Ain't you heaven-sent?*—He says, *Dammit I'm just a baby and
this crown is so heavy.* When we ask Him where He came from if it's not
the Land on High of Milk and Honey, He just says, *I come from the same
dark place as you.* Then he licks clean the middle of an Oreo and cries
for the lack of milk to wash it down.

The All-Star

Indeed, indeed: Our Father was a schoolboy football hero. Hand Him the ball and watch Him run. He could punch through any line, scalpel through an All-State secondary. He of the Crazy Legs, His was the stiffest of Stiff Arms. We sometimes wonder why Daddy didn't just keep running, never look back. When each of us was a little bit younger, He tested us out: *Take this here pigskin and run straight through me.* When He stuffed us, each one, He seemed to breathe easier, to puff His chest, poke out His derriere, even as He said, S'alright: *not everybody's meant for gridiron glory. There's no shame in it.*

He'd even dust us off and pat our behinds. *Get you an iced treat from your mother. Tell her you been playing ball with Dear Old Dad.* Of course, that was hit or miss: sometimes there were treats, most times not. Always Mother would mumble: *Wish you wouldn't encourage him.* But Baby-Boy, now that's different. Mother tells her youngest boy, *Go show him what you're made of, Child.* And he does. He is just a Tyke when Our Father takes him out to scrimmage. The little Dynamo takes his stance and revs his engines. The dark gray sky roils above. The One Pale Sycamore is leafless and bony. Perfect weather for a scrum.

Hut one, hut two, HIKE! When the dust settles, Our Father is a dead-grass heap in the yard, and Baby-Boy is still a blur, running, running down the street. When he crests the hill he stops and turns and waves. *I shall return,* he shouts down to us. *Be your best good selves 'til I get back.* Then he's gone.

Charon's Boat

Ding-dong, the King is dead. Or something like it anyway. Our Father, once an able-bodied sort, has taken unkindly to his plight. What it is, he won't say, but he's not been the same since our Youngest's recent exodus. He sits in the chair, eats his suppers on a TV tray—lunch and breakfast too. Mother sits with him all night, as if it is a dream come true. She's buoyed up by something, says such things are wont to happen to a man, such as this modern age tends to be. There's books about it. Talk shows too. *When a man comes to know his limits, he's got hell to pay.* She brings him beers, pats him on the shoulder. *There, there, Dear.* Sometimes, though, we catch her biting her knuckle to hold the giggles in. And he is a nightmare scene: stubble, catatonia, man-funk, frozen foods, the blue-blare TV screen at all hours. We shush ourselves one night, sneak through the kitchen to the garage. There's our steed, a vessel to deliver us: the Gremlin. We'd fire it up, if we knew how, if it wouldn't make an infernal racket. So we don't. It's a clandestine mission instead. Up goes the door, quiet, underneath the living room blare. In we climb, all of us, and the Rusted Monster sags beneath us. Those of us who are heartier, we push. Down the little driveway, aiming at whatever descending slopes the neighborhood can offer. The night breeze rushes by. Gravity pushes us along. None of us has ever gone this fast, this far. We speed down, down to whatever end's in store.

Communion

She is our mother. In her mixing bowl, she stirs lump crab. Green peppers. Red peppers. Mayonnaise. This is the way she celebrates.

Danny and I go to the harbor. It stinks. The air is cold. No snow. If there was snow it would be different, but there is no snow. The harbor is dark and it stinks. Danny stares across it.

—What are you looking at? I ask

—The Domino sign.

The Domino Sugars sign is bright red against the black sky and the black harbor. The lower part of the D is out, but every other letter shines hot in our field of vision.

—Ma's crazy, I say.

—She's old.

—She's not that old.

—She's not that crazy.

We get up and walk down the harbor, into the neighborhoods. We don't say anything and it gets darker back there. Danny's Escort is parked two blocks away. I don't let myself get scared. Danny might be scared, I don't know.

—There's crab cakes when we get back.

—There is. Yeah.

†

Hannah and Mary and Zadie wrap presents. Zadie's are fat with paper, round. They're not crisp the way presents should be. Hannah and Mary shout at her.

—Do it right.

—They're my presents, you shits.

—Fine, monkey.

They have always called each other monkey. It means many things. Like Chinese or some other language: the way you say it is everything. In this case it means, *You're right but so am I.*

Danny doesn't have to ask where we can find our mother. She's in the kitchen. I follow him. He opens the ice box and grabs a Mickey's. He hands one to me. I don't want it but I stare down at that green, wide-mouthed bottle and try not to look up.

—Ma?

She mixes. A big steel bowl and a fat-handled ladle. The white meat and the diced peppers, green and red.

—Yeah, hon, she says. I'm mixing the cakes.

—That's good. They gonna be ready soon?

—Soon enough. Yeah, soon.

Danny gets up to leave.

—No, stay, she says. Keep me company.

—Richie'll stay, Ma. I gotta keep those girls from stabbing each other with the scissors.

Danny doesn't look back. Our mother looks over at me and smiles. I see her one milky eye and the other clear one. The clear one stares at me, knows me as the small lump she held close all those years ago. The milky eye is dead to anything and it stares past me. She digs her hands into the bowl of meat and rolls it into tiny ovals, pats those down to disks and dusts them with flour and cornmeal.

—Why don't you get me a frying pan ready, Rich. At first she doesn't look up from her patties, but when I don't get up immediately, she looks over.

—Rich? Come on. Help your mother. You look like I got a canker.

So I do it. I don't want to do it, but I do it. The cast iron is heavy, lands with a clank on the burner. I pour the oil.

—Not that much, kiddo, she tells me, and I stop pouring.

She turns on the burner. We stand above the pan, waiting for the oil to heat. Our mother starts to her mumbling. The hair on the back of my neck stands on end. I feel hot in my cheeks. She says the Lord's prayer, crosses herself, pulls a safety pin from her apron pocket and pricks her left-hand ring finger. She raises it to the air.

—We miss you, Frankie. The kids love you, I love you. Look out for us.

She motions for me to drop the first cakes into the oil. They snap to. As they begin to cook, this woman, our mother, takes her thumb and pricked ring finger together and squeezes a dark drop of herself onto each soft, white mound.

TJ Beitelman is the author of a novel, *John the Revelator*, as well as two collections of poetry, *In Order to Form a More Perfect Union* and *Americana*, all from Black Lawrence Press. He's also published a hybrid memoir, *Self-Helpless: A Misfit's Guide to Life, Liberty, and the Pursuit of Happiness*, which is available from Outpost 19. His stories and poems have appeared widely in literary magazines, and he's received fellowships from the Alabama State Council on the Arts and the Cultural Alliance of Greater Birmingham. He taught writing and literature at Virginia Tech, where he earned an M.A. in English, and at the University of Alabama, where he earned an M.F.A. in creative writing and also edited *Black Warrior Review*. He currently directs the creative writing program at the Alabama School of Fine Arts in Birmingham and can be found online at www.tjbman.com.